ABOUT THE AUTHOR

Catherine Coles has written stories since the day she could form sentences, she can barely believe that making things up in her head classes as work!! Catherine lives in the north east of England where she shares her home with her children and two spoiled dogs who have no idea they are not human! She loves to hear from readers at catherine@catherinecoles.com.

Books by Catherine Coles

Murder at the Manor
Murder at the Village Fete
Murder in the Churchyard
Murder in Belgrave Square
Murder at the Wedding Chapel

Visit Catherine's website for the most up to date information
www.catherinecoles.com

MURDER IN BELGRAVE SQUARE

CATHERINE COLES

INSPIRED PRESS LIMITED

INSPIRED PRESS LIMITED
ISBN: 978-1-8384411-4-2
Murder in Belgrave Square

Editor: Sara Miller
Book design: Sally Clements
www.catherinecoles.com

CAST OF CHARACTERS

Main Characters

Tommy Christie – The 7th Earl of Northmoor, former police officer
Evelyn Christie – Policewoman during the Great War, Tommy's wife

The Family

Lady Emily Christie – Tommy's great-aunt
Lady Victoria Bernard – Tommy's aunt
Elise Bernard – Lady Victoria's eldest daughter
Madeleine Bernard – Lady Victoria's younger daughter

The Guests

Frederick Ryder – The 9th Earl of Chesden and an old family friend
Sarah Ryder – His wife
Alexander Ryder – The Earl's eldest son
David Ryder – The Earl's younger son
Hugh Norton-Cavendish – Alexander & David's school friend

The Staff

Wilfred Malton - The butler
Phyllis Chapman - The housekeeper
Mary O'Connell - The cook
Walter Davies - Tommy's valet

Frank Douglas - First Footman
Arthur Brown - Second Footman
Gladys Ferriby - Lady Emily's lady's maid
Doris - Evelyn's maid
Alice Morrison – wet nurse
Ada Burrows – nursemaid

Others

Georges Dubois – Madeleine's beau
Detective Chief Inspector Price – detective in charge of
investigating the murder
Detective Sergeant Harrington – junior detective
Herbert Michaels – family doctor

CHAPTER 1

*B*elgrave Square, London – April 1922

"*T*he newspaper says the *Majestic* leaves from Southampton next month," Tommy commented nonchalantly.

"If you want to take a holiday and sail to New York, why don't you just say so?" Evelyn smiled at her husband of eight years.

Tall and broad shouldered, with blond hair, he was a jolly decent looking fellow even if she said so herself. When they married immediately before the commencement of the war, Tommy worked for the North Yorkshire police. Back then he had been plain old Thomas Christie. Now, thanks to a combination of military conflicts, Spanish flu, and murderous relatives, he was Lord Northmoor.

Inheriting a title and a grand home hadn't changed Tommy one bit. He would do almost anything to make her happy and rarely made her question whether he adored her as much now as he undoubtedly had the day they married.

"I would if I thought you would actually accompany me on such a trip. I don't imagine they take animals on board." He looked pointedly at the dog bed in the corner of their bedroom.

Nancy, her beloved Gordon Setter, lay on a thick plaid blanket along with Mary, a puppy from her litter earlier that year curled up next to her snoring softly. Davey, the puppy Tommy had bought for her birthday the previous summer, now a young adult, was at home in Yorkshire. He was a mischievous animal with a penchant for stealing items of clothing and making a mad dash for it across the manor house's expansive gardens. Evelyn's mother was looking after him alongside her own pack of dogs.

"What's in New York that we can't get in Hessleham?" she asked, only half joking.

Tommy looked at her over the top of the newspaper. "Where is your sense of adventure, darling?"

"Thomas Christie!" she exclaimed. "I don't know how you can say such a thing after the puzzles we've been involved with."

"Puzzles?" Tommy folded his paper and looked at her with a raised eyebrow. "Those were murders. And cold-blooded murders at that. Danger isn't at all the same thing as adventures."

"Whatever you want to call it, I've had enough over the last year. All I want is a nice, quiet life free from drama."

He chuckled. "And your solution is to come to London at the start of the Season? Don't you remember what that was like when you were a debutante?"

Evelyn grimaced. It was about as peaceful as Petticoat Lane Market. She had not enjoyed being paraded about at dinners, parties, and other social events in the hope some man would find her so enchanting he would propose. She much preferred the quieter life in village of Hessleham.

"It was awful. I couldn't wait to return home to carry on

2

helping my mother with the dogs. I found them much easier to deal with than people."

"I think you'd still rather spend your time with your dogs than most humans." Tommy observed.

"All humans are not equal, my dear." Evelyn got up from the seat in front of the mirror where she'd been putting the last touches to her makeup for the evening. "You, for example, are a quite splendid specimen."

He reached up and pulled her down to sit on his lap. "I can remember many times when you didn't think I was as marvellous as you do now."

Evelyn chuckled. "I don't think there are many women who would be enamoured of a man who is attempting to arrest them."

Tommy shrugged. "You were, so far as I could see, breaking and entering in a residential property. That was, and still is, a crime."

She smiled at their humble beginnings. On the night in question, Evelyn and her sister, Milly, had returned home from an evening at the pictures. Their mother, so busy with one of her labouring bitches, had forgotten her daughters were not home and had locked them out.

Evelyn had helped Milly climb through an upstairs window and was preparing to do so herself when Tommy had blasted a shrill note on his whistle. It was still a complete mystery to her how she hadn't toppled from the ladder into the flowerbed below.

"I'm still amazed you thought arresting a girl was the way to win her heart."

He grinned. "It worked though, didn't it?"

As she snuggled in his arms, one of her very favourite places in the world, she couldn't argue. Evelyn reached up and put a hand on his cheek. "I've never been happier."

Of course, there was one thing that would make both of them feel even happier. Some months ago, after solving their last murder, they had both agreed that talking about their childlessness only made it more painful.

In the past few months, Evelyn's sister had recently given birth to twin girls—Leonora and Eleanor, Nancy had ten puppies, and their dear friends Teddy and Isolde Mainwaring had married and were expecting their first child in the summer.

Tommy bent his head and kissed Evelyn. The familiar warmth spread through her belly, and she wished everything in life was as uncomplicated as the love she felt for her husband.

"Much as I wish we could stay here like this for the rest of the evening," he said. "I think if we don't go down for dinner soon, my aunt will send a search party."

They had arrived in London earlier that day and briefly met Tommy's Aunt Victoria and her daughters, Elise and Madeleine.

A sharp rap on the door sounded, and Evelyn pushed herself up from Tommy's knee and touched up her lipstick. She patted her black hair, even though it still looked as perfect as it had when Doris finished styling it earlier.

"Come in!" Tommy called.

"Would you like me to sit with Nancy and Mary now?" Doris asked.

"Your timing is excellent," Evelyn replied. "Lord Northmoor and I are ready to go down for dinner. Thank you."

Doris had worked for Evelyn since she had married Tommy. The maid had been Evelyn's constant companion through the war years, from the early months when they had all believed the war would be over quickly, to the last months when Tommy was missing somewhere in France, to when he returned to Hessleham injured.

They maintained the expected professional relationship in public, but privately were much less formal. Doris had been with Evelyn through the darkest times of her life and would always be closer to her than an ordinary employee as a result.

Tommy put out an arm. "Lady Northmoor."

She looped her arm through his. "Lord Northmoor."

He always seemed to know when she needed a little extra support and his cool reassurance.

Evelyn took one last glance at the puppy fast asleep beside its mother and wished she could stay and watch over her instead of Doris. Sometimes being dutiful was much harder than she had ever imagined.

~

*T*ommy looked at his wife as they descended the stairs. "I think I forgot to tell you how exquisite you look this evening."

They were not simply empty words. Doris had piled Evelyn's very dark hair at the back of her head in intricate waves. A dress of a colour he guessed had a fancy name that Evelyn had told him, but he'd promptly forgotten, encased her petite form. All he knew was that it was the exact same yellow as the dahlias the gardener grew at Hessleham Hall.

She smiled up at him, but he recognised it for the empty gesture it was. Evelyn was struggling to maintain her usual cheerful nature. He hoped some time away from home would do her some good. Perhaps being away from her sister and Isolde, both of whom had what Evelyn so desperately wanted, would help.

"You would say that if I had just returned from a particularly blustery walk along the seafront with the dogs."

"I expect I would say something like, you looked charming with your rosy cheeks and windswept hair. That's not quite the same as exquisite."

Evelyn patted his hand but did not reply. He wished he had the right words to say to comfort her.

Apparently six months was not a particularly long time to wait to be blessed with a child. His friend, the village doctor, Teddy Mainwaring, had reassured him of that. However, that was of very little consolation to Evelyn, given Teddy and Isolde had conceived a child quickly. So swiftly, in fact, that their wedding was a very rushed affair given Isolde was already carrying their baby.

They reached the drawing room, and he opened the door for Evelyn.

"At last," Aunt Em said from her seat on the sofa next to the fire. "I thought you had abandoned me, and I was to eat alone this evening."

Tommy looked at the clock on the mantlepiece. "Are we so very late, Aunt Em?"

"It's after seven," she admonished. "Do you young people require a gong to let you know the time?"

"Shall we have a drink?" he said briskly.

His great-aunt was usually forthright, and a well-known plain speaker, but she seemed particularly edgy that evening.

"Is there something wrong?" Evelyn asked, sitting next to Em.

"I don't suppose it's anything a gin and tonic will not fix." Em nodded at Malton, the butler.

"My Lady. Lord Northmoor, Lady Northmoor, will you both take a drink?"

"Nothing for me, thank you." Tommy turned to Evelyn. "My dear?"

"I will join Lady Emily in a gin and tonic please, Malton."

He turned to the drink cabinet and poured their drinks. As was his way, Malton unobtrusively placed a small table near Emily and Evelyn and placed their drinks on its smooth surface.

"I understand our guests arrived this afternoon?"

"That is correct, Aunt Em." Tommy stood near the fire

facing his aunt and wife. "You remember Lord Chesden, I am sure?"

"Indeed." Aunt Em took a sip of her drink. "I believe he was a friend of Charles."

Charles was the eldest child of Emily's brother, Edward. "That is correct. He is here with his wife, Sarah, and their sons, Alexander and David."

"They also asked if an old school chum of theirs could stay too. A Hugh Norton-Cavendish."

"Surely they are no longer schoolboys?" Aunt Em raised an eyebrow in surprise. "I had believed Lord Chesden's sons to be in their twenties."

"Indeed, they are," Tommy agreed. "However, Hugh was keen to stay with friends. Apparently, his family is away on the continent, and his father didn't want to open up their London house for just Hugh."

"I imagine that is a euphemism for the Norton-Cavendish's being unable to stretch their finances," Aunt Em suggested tartly as she took a sip of her gin and tonic.

"I'm sure..." Evelyn began.

"No." Tommy grimaced. "I'm afraid Aunt Em is quite correct. The word is that Harold Norton-Cavendish likes the horses a little too much. I imagine they have sent poor Hugh out to find himself a rich young wife to save his family's fortunes."

"How dreadful," Evelyn murmured.

"Scandalous," Em agreed, finishing her drink. "I think I shall have another, Malton."

"Of course, My Lady." Malton looked to Evelyn. "Lady Northmoor?"

"Not for me, I have barely touched this one."

The door opened, and Victoria Bernard entered. Her fair hair, a feature of the Christie family, was still more blonde than grey and despite being in her late fifties, she was still a very attractive woman.

Victoria had left Hessleham Hall as a young woman to run away to France and marry a penniless painter. It was said her husband, Louis, had ruined the reputation of more than one young lady before he met Victoria and persuaded her to elope with him. Her father, then Lord Northmoor, had been so furious with his only daughter he had disowned her, and they had never spoken again.

When Victoria had written to Tommy asking if she and her daughters may stay in the family's London house, he had not hesitated. Aunt Em had spoken fondly of her niece, and he was certain it was she who had persuaded Victoria to seek the help of her family.

"The girls will be down soon." Victoria took a seat opposite Em and Evelyn. "Madeleine's maid tells me she's had some problem with her gown. You know how young girls are. They want everything to be just so. Particularly when there are young men in attendance."

"I understand from Lord Northmoor that one of Lord Chesden's sons is fond of Madeleine?"

Victoria beamed. "She hasn't yet been presented at court, and she has already made a favourable impression on one of the oldest and most respected families in the country. This is the very reason I brought Elise and Madeleine over to England."

"Is Elise rather cross that she is to be left out?" Aunt Em wondered.

"Elise is too old to be presented." Victoria looked at her aunt through narrowed eyes. "She understands that."

Although Victoria had asked for somewhere to stay, she had not asked for anything else. She had received the legacy left to her by her brother, Charles. Tommy rather thought the reason only one of his aunt's daughters was enjoying a London Season was because her inheritance would only cover the expenses for one child.

It was probably too late for him to offer to pay for Elise to have the same opportunities as her sister. He would talk to Evelyn later and see what her thoughts were on the matter. She would probably have a much better idea of how these things worked than he did.

The drawing-room door suddenly burst open with a loud crash. A young man scanned the area, then looked behind him before approaching Victoria.

"Where is she?" he asked in rapid French.

Victoria replied so quickly that Tommy's rudimentary grasp of French wasn't able to translate and understand her response.

Evelyn got to her feet and stood next to Tommy. "I apologise. I didn't catch your name. May I introduce my husband, Lord Northmoor? He and Madeleine Bernard, whom I believe you are looking for, are cousins."

She spoke careful French in quiet, reassuring tones. Tommy admired the way his wife took charge of a volatile situation with gentle authority.

"Georges Dubois…"

"My Lady," Malton inserted. "You should address Lady Northmoor as 'My Lady'."

Tommy stepped forward and extended his hand. "Pleased to meet you."

"Malton." Evelyn looked at the butler, "Will you please see that another place is set for dinner?"

His expression was doubtful, but he would never express any misgivings he might hold. "Certainly, My Lady."

Georges glanced at Tommy and then at his own clothes. "I do not think…"

"Nonsense," Tommy said firmly. "You have travelled all the way from France to see Madeleine. Of course you must eat with us. Now, I am sure you would like a drink?"

He drew Georges over to the cabinet as Malton left the room.

"Take that look off your face, dear," Aunt Em said. "I have

told you many times in my letters that Tommy and Evelyn are very decent people."

"But Lord Chesden," Victoria wailed. "What will he think?"

"He will think whatever we tell him," Em said imperiously.

Tommy grinned as he poured a generous measure of brandy for himself and another for Georges.

"Which is?" Victoria demanded.

"Georges is a young man hopelessly infatuated with Madeleine, and we, as polite members of society, are honour bound to give the young man a place to stay given he has travelled so far."

"But to sit at the table and eat dinner with us?"

Georges gulped down his drink. "I will not eat with the fine English ladies and gentlemen."

"I insist," Tommy said.

The door opened again, and Elise and Madeleine entered.

"Georges!" she cried.

"My darling," he responded, holding out his arms to her.

Madeleine looked at her mother, then back to Georges. "Come with me. You must wait in the kitchen."

Elise giggled. "Oh dear, what will Alexander Ryder think of this?"

Madeleine beckoned Georges to follow her. As she opened the door, Lord Chesden walked through, his cane tapping on the floor with each step.

"Who do we have here?" he asked in his booming voice.

"Temporary London staff," Aunt Em said in a bored voice. "They don't know one floor of the house from another."

"Why is young Madeleine showing him where to go?" Frederick Ryder asked as he shook his head. "What a peculiar setup you have here, Northmoor."

"We pride ourselves on adapting to all situations." Evelyn got to her feet. "Do you take brandy before dinner?"

Lord Chesden sat down heavily on a chair near the door. "I blame the war. One could get decent help before that. A countess shouldn't be serving her guests pre-dinner drinks. It's simply not done."

Evelyn poured a brandy and took it over. "I think you'll find us a very modern couple. I hope that doesn't shock you too much, Lord Chesden."

"I suppose one has to adjust to modern times," he said doubtfully.

Privately, Tommy thought his wife serving Lord Chesden a drink was much less impolite than the fact the man's wife and sons had not yet arrived downstairs. The older man was too similar to his now deceased Uncle Charles for Tommy's liking.

"Not quite the excitement you were expecting," Aunt Em said to Evelyn with a devilish smile.

"No," Evelyn agreed. "Intrigue rather seems to follow us about."

~

Weariness surrounded Evelyn like a heavy cloak. She couldn't remember a time she had last felt so completely exhausted. Dinner was a trial. Frederick Ryder was hard work. He dominated conversation—whether he was speaking to someone next to him or at the other end of the table.

Before she knew it, they would do it all over again at breakfast.

"You look done in," Tommy whispered, taking her hand. "Let's excuse ourselves and go to bed."

"Can we?" She looked at their guests.

"It's my house, so I say yes."

It wasn't very often that Tommy pulled his 'Lord of the manor' act as Evelyn called it. Usually, he downplayed his title and the corresponding benefits it came with. He hated to think people treated him differently simply because of the family he was born into.

"We've had a terribly long day," Tommy said to their guests. "Lady Northmoor and I are ready to retire. The travelling has exhausted us."

Aunt Em got to her feet with surprising speed for a lady her age. "I shall walk upstairs with you."

"This is London!" Fred Ryder barked. "No one goes to sleep at this early hour."

"We do," Tommy said firmly.

"Your behaviour is very extraordinary."

"I'm certain it seems so to you," Tommy agreed pleasantly. "Good evening."

He opened the door for his aunt.

Fred Ryder's strident voice followed them. "I do hope someone has remembered to tell your cook I like my toast done extremely lightly. I can't abide toast that is too dark."

"Of course, Lord Chesden." Evelyn inclined her head before she hurried from the room.

"What an obnoxious man," Aunt Em said, as Tommy closed the door firmly behind them.

"You said he was an old family friend," Tommy protested. "Perhaps I would not have agreed to his visit if you hadn't told me that."

"And so he is," Aunt Em agreed. "Well, that is to say, his family and our family have been friends for generations. My brother, Edward, and Fred's father were extremely close. I think Charles and Fred are cut from the same cloth, which probably explains their friendship."

Evelyn sighed. "I should speak to Mrs O'Connell about Lord Chesden's toast preferences. If we get it wrong, he's the type of man to tell everyone he meets that our hospitality is not up to snuff"

"I expect he will do that, anyway." Tommy stopped

walking as they reached the foot of the stairs. "We have left him and his family with only Victoria for company."

Em frowned. "Where did the girls go? They seemed to disappear quickly after dinner."

"I believe Madeleine said she had invites to respond to," Evelyn said. "Elise said something about a headache."

"She excused herself not long after that fellow Norton-Cavendish." Tommy caught hold of Evelyn's arm. "I say, do you think there might be something going on between those two?"

Evelyn thought about it for a moment. "I didn't think they had met each other before this evening."

"As if that stops young people these days," Em scoffed. "Certainly your investigations in the past have shown that very few people seem to be satisfied with their spouse these days."

"Sadly, that seems to be true." Tommy looked at Evelyn. "Why don't you give Doris the message about Chesden's toast to pass on to Cook?"

"That's a fine idea," Evelyn said brightly. "Why didn't I think of that?"

"Because you're jolly tired and practically asleep on your feet. Shall I carry you up?"

Evelyn was almost certain he was joking, but sometimes it was very hard to tell with Tommy. "You will scandalise your aunt talking like that!"

"It takes an awful lot more than a husband carrying his wife up some stairs to scandalise me," Em said with a sly grin. "Now whether you are walking or being carried, may we get moving?"

Tommy stood to his aunt's right and held out his arm for her to use for support as she climbed the stairs, her left hand resting on the bannister. Evelyn made a note to speak to Em about her hips when they were alone. She wouldn't embarrass Em by speaking of her infirmities in front of Tommy.

They saw Em to her room and then went to their own suite. Doris was sitting by the fire, the book she had been reading in her lap. Her mouth was slightly open and soft snores filled the room.

Tommy snapped the door shut with a sharp click. Doris startled and jumped to her feet. "Goodness, My Lady, I wasn't expecting you back so soon. I closed my eyes for only a minute."

"Doris, we've all had a long day. I'm hardly going to reprimand you for taking a nap when exhaustion is the very reason we are retiring early ourselves."

Tommy went through to his own room so his valet could help him get ready for bed. Doris helped Evelyn out of her dress. Mary moved over to sniff Evelyn's toes. She bent down and picked the puppy up. "Have you been a good girl for Doris?"

Doris smiled indulgently. She was quite used to hearing her mistress talk to her dogs as though they were human.

"She has been a delight," Doris confirmed. "Perhaps I should take her out one last time?"

"If you don't mind, that is a good idea."

Before Doris left the room, Evelyn passed on the message about Lord Chesden's requirements for his toast in the morning.

Evelyn finished getting ready for bed, and Tommy joined her. He patted Nancy's head. "Where's Mary?"

"Doris has taken her out," Evelyn said. "She should be back at any moment."

Running footsteps sounded in the hall. "That can't be her."

Frantic knocking on their door brought Nancy to the foot of the bed. Her tail swished from side to side, letting Evelyn know that whoever was outside was someone she knew.

Tommy walked over to the door and opened it. "Oh, Lord Northmoor!"

"Doris, what on earth is the matter?"

"I took Mary outside…" Doris panted, then looked at Evelyn in horror. "I've left the puppy in the courtyard."

Evelyn got out of bed and pulled her wrap around her. "You look quite ill. What happened outside?"

"There's a man on the kitchen step." Doris shook her head in dismay. "My Lady, I think he's dead."

CHAPTER 2

"*I*s this man inside or outside the house?" Tommy asked calmly.

"Outside, My Lord, he fell to the side when I opened the door."

"And Mary?"

"She scampered off to do her business, and I'm afraid I screamed rather loudly and ran inside. I'm so sorry I forgot all about the puppy."

"There's only one thing for it." Tommy thrust his feet into his bedroom slippers and pulled on his robe. "I shall have to check on this fellow and call the police."

Evelyn opened a drawer and took out a pair of socks. She quickly put them on, then put her feet into her boots. "I'll come with you."

He nodded. "I knew you would."

Tommy led the way back down the corridor to the stairs. Evelyn put an arm around Doris's shoulders. Her maid was shaking, her pallor paler than Evelyn's nightgown.

When they reached the kitchen, Evelyn pulled out a chair. "Sit here now. When I return, I'll make you a cup of tea."

Doris did as she was bid. She looked at Evelyn but said nothing. Her maid was obviously suffering from shock.

"That door?" Tommy asked, his voice low and reassuring, as he indicated a door at the end of a passageway just outside the kitchen.

Doris nodded. Her hands trembled where she rested them on the table. She looked down at them, then folded them in her lap. Tears shone in her eyes.

"We'll be as quick as we can," Evelyn told her and followed Tommy toward the door.

He pulled it open to reveal a man laid across the step. His feet rested on the ground as though he had sat for a rest before keeling over. Tommy stepped over him and stood in the courtyard. Mary ran over to him and jumped excitedly at his pyjama bottoms. She then ran to the dead man and sniffed at something on the ground, her tail wagging with excitement.

Picking her up, he carefully leaned across the victim to transfer the dog into Evelyn's arms.

"Do you recognise him?"

Tommy put one knee on the step and peered into the victim's face. "It's Georges."

"Are you sure?"

"I'm afraid so," he said. "There's an obvious stab wound to his chest."

"Is he dead?"

"Most definitely." Tommy stood up and stepped back. "Are there any candles in the kitchen? There's something behind his legs and I can't see what it is. It's too dark."

She went into the kitchen and gave a wriggling Mary to Doris. Turning on the stove, she filled the kettle and put it over the heat to boil.

Opening drawers, she quickly found what she was looking for. She put a candle into a holder and lit it. With a hand around the flame so it didn't blow out, she took it to Tommy.

"What is it?"

"It appears to be a basket. I think there's a kitten inside. Can't you hear that noise?"

She shook her head. He reached out, took hold of the edge of the wicker container, and pulled it towards him.

"Tommy, you shouldn't touch anything before the police arrive!" Evelyn exclaimed as the carrier came into view. She put a hand over her mouth. "Oh, my goodness."

Wrapped in a shawl was a baby.

He looked up at her, thoughts running around in his head so fast they bumped into each other. "I was expecting a cat."

Evelyn knelt beside the basket and lifted the infant out. The crocheted shawl appeared to be the only thing covering the child's naked body. "I think she's a newborn."

Tears sprang to Evelyn's eyes as she cradled the baby in her arms. Tommy couldn't understand who would do such a thing? Or why? Was it Georges's baby? Had someone placed the baby next to the doorstep before or after his murder?

He put his arm around Evelyn's shoulders and drew her back inside the house. "Let's get both of you warm. I shall telephone for the police."

Doris jumped to her feet as Tommy and Evelyn walked back into the kitchen.

"Oh, My Lady! What on earth is going on this evening?" Doris put Mary on the floor and lifted the whistling kettle from the stove. "I will make the tea. You should take the baby and sit in the drawing room. After I have brought a tray through, I will re-light the fire."

"You've had a terrible shock," Evelyn rested a hand on Doris's arm. "Are you sure you feel up to it?"

Doris's smile was wobbly, but she squared her shoulders and nodded at her mistress. "Of course, My Lady. I will see to the tea and the puppy."

Tommy picked up a heavy blanket resting on the chair next to the fire. A thought occurred to him before he left the kitchen. "Are there still guests in the drawing room?"

"We left Victoria with the entire Ryder family less than an hour ago." Evelyn tucked the shawl more securely around the infant. "Surely they will still be there?"

"We shall go to the library, Doris. Of course, everyone will know something is amiss when the police arrive. Until then, I would prefer for us to at least attempt to keep what has happened quiet."

"Of course, My Lord.

Tommy led the way to the library. When Evelyn had settled herself and the infant in the chair nearest to the barely warm fireplace, Tommy secured the cover around them both.

"Who would do such a thing?" Evelyn wondered as she gazed into the face of the baby. He watched as the baby's bright blue eyes stared right back at his wife.

With a sinking heart, Tommy knew Evelyn wasn't referring to the murder of Georges. She only had eyes and concern for the child in her arms. As he left the room, Evelyn was whispering words of reassurance to the baby and promises that she herself would take good care of her. Exactly what he feared. The infant would completely capture Evelyn's soft heart before the police even arrived.

He placed a call to the local police, then went to wake Malton.

The faithful family butler was the most likely person to know if the attic of the house held anything they could use for the baby. Tommy was aware of most things held in storage at Hessleham Hall, but he did not know what their town house in Belgrave Square might hold.

Even as he made plans to make the baby as comfortable as possible during her stay at his house, Tommy couldn't help but think even that was a big mistake. It would encourage Evelyn to become attached to the child.

Despite the look of pure joy on her face, he should tell the police to find somewhere else for the baby to live as soon as they arrived. If he didn't, it would only cause more anguish in the future.

~

*B*y the time the police arrived, Evelyn and Mrs Chapman had bathed the baby and they dressed her in clean clothes. As soon as the shops opened in the morning, she vowed to buy the child a completely new wardrobe.

"Go over that again," Detective Chief Inspector Price demanded in his nasally voice. "I am especially interested in the part where you both thought it would be a good idea to tamper with evidence in what was clearly a murder enquiry."

"You cannot think the baby has anything to do with the murder of Mr Dubois," Evelyn protested.

"From what your husband has told us, Lady Northmoor, the basket holding the child was underneath the body of the victim."

"It's not entirely accurate to say 'underneath the body'," Tommy corrected. "Mr Dubois was half sitting, half slumped on the back step, as you have seen. We have not touched him. He is in the exact same position as he was when we found him. The carrier containing the baby was on the ground next to the step. It doesn't follow that the two things are linked."

"You say you worked as a detective before the war, Lord Northmoor?"

"I did."

"Were you particularly successful?"

Evelyn worked to keep her face straight. Too many people assumed Tommy had received benefits because of his title. It often led to him being underestimated.

"Successful enough to know not to jump to conclusions within the first half hour of an investigation," Tommy replied smartly. "If he was killed because of something to do with the baby, why was she left? We don't know if the baby was his, someone else's, or there because of entirely different circumstances to those which ended in Mr Dubois's murder."

"But to answer your original question," Evelyn added. "My husband did not think it prudent to leave a newborn infant without adequate protection from the elements in our courtyard late at night. If he had, the body of Georges Dubois might not have been the only one you're investigating."

"I'll see to it that the child is transported to the nearest workhouse as soon as I can," he muttered. The detective looked slightly chastened as he moved over and peered down at the baby sleeping in Evelyn's arms. "It looks healthy enough."

"*She*," Evelyn said frostily. "Will not be taken to any workhouse."

"Lady Northmoor?"

"The baby will stay here with me until you find her parents." She stared hard at the man until his cheeks flushed with colour. "Presumably you will make enquiries to determine her parents given you believe the crimes are connected?"

"Perhaps we should put an advertisement in the newspaper, sir?" Detective Sergeant Harrington suggested brightly.

"How would we phrase that?" Price asked scathingly. "Abandoned baby: enquire within. The Northmoors would have every desperate childless couple within miles of central London on their doorstep."

Evelyn flinched as she gazed at the baby's face. She lifted a hand and smoothed down the little girl's downy blonde hair. Was that what she was? So desperate to care for a child she was latching on to this child as though it was her only hope of being a mother? "So that is settled. There will be no more talk of the workhouse."

"My wife is correct." Tommy put down the cup of tea he

wasn't drinking and walked over to the sideboard. Lifting the decanter, he poured a measure of brandy into a glass and took a healthy swallow. "Neither of us would allow this baby to be taken to the workhouse when we can care for her ourselves. It is our Christian duty."

Evelyn raised an eyebrow at Tommy's unusually pious words. "It will also be my absolute pleasure."

"Back to the murder." Price looked at his colleague. "Harrington found part of a bank note in the dead man's hand. That leads me to believe the motive for this murder is some sort of gambling dispute, or blackmail."

"How would either of those motives involve this baby?" Evelyn demanded. She might not be the child's mother, but she would care for, and defend her, as though she was. It was the least she could do while she had care of the precious little mite.

"Maybe the baby was part of the wager." Price shrugged. "The scrap of paper we found was part of a fifty-pound note."

"Dubois must have won the gamble." Tommy drank the rest of his brandy and put the glass down next to the decanter. Evelyn didn't doubt that he would need more of the amber liquid before the police allowed them to retire for the evening. "What sort of bet would win a fellow money and a baby?"

"A rather odd one, I agree, but who knows what goes on at illegal gambling games." Price looked around the room, taking in the high ceilings, polished floors, and pictures of unknown ancestors. They go on all over the city. In the backrooms of pubs, warehouses, and even private residences."

"Let me see if I am following your thought processes correctly." Tommy moved across the room to stand in front of the detective. "Dubois won a bet. He must have, because he had money torn from his dying grip. For reasons unknown, that wager involved a baby."

Price cleared his throat. "It does sound rather improbable."

"Impossible, I would suggest," Evelyn said. "This baby is only hours old. They had not even bathed her following her birth. Perhaps you would allow us to telephone our family doctor so he can examine the child and confirm what I am telling you?"

"At the moment all we have is theories," he said pompously. "We will search for any other evidence there may be."

"You have my permission to search any of the downstairs rooms you please." Tommy moved over to Evelyn and placed a hand on her shoulder. "You may also speak with my wife's maid, Doris, who is in the kitchen with our housekeeper and butler. As the other staff rise for the day, you may speak to them."

"But...My Lord," Price protested. "It is the middle of the night. You surely don't intend for us to stay here until morning?"

"If that is not acceptable to you," Tommy responded. "I will allow my staff to go to bed and ensure they are available to you at such time in the morning as you may return."

"We must maintain the integrity of the crime scene," Price replied stiffly. "No one must leave or come into the house until we are satisfied our investigations are complete."

"Other than our doctor," Evelyn interjected. "I insist upon that."

"Who else is in the house now?"

"My Aunt Em, an older lady in her eighties. My Aunt Victoria, who is in her fifties. Her daughters Madeleine and Elise. Family friends, Frederick Ryder, his wife Sarah, and their sons Alexander and David. Finally, a school chum of the Ryder boys named Hugh Norton-Cavendish. Of course, we also have a number of staff here too."

"Are all the guests in bed?" Harrington asked.

"I can't be sure," Tommy answered. "They are our guests and as such are not required to retire at the same time on an evening as my wife and I retire."

"We will speak to everyone who is awake." Detective Inspector Price marched to the library door. "It would have been helpful if you had told us before now some of your guests may still be awake."

"You didn't ask." Tommy squeezed Evelyn's shoulder. "And I didn't want to interfere. After all, you're the detective."

∾

"*H*e did rather ask for that." Evelyn smiled as Tommy re-entered the library after he'd shown the detectives to the drawing room and telephoned for the doctor.

He pulled a face. "It aggravates me that people hear my title and then write me off as a brainless buffoon."

"Poor darling," Evelyn consoled. "Whatever are we to do about everything?"

Tommy grinned as he sat in the chair opposite. "What we always do. We shall investigate and solve both crimes. On this occasion, I am particularly keen that we uncover the murderer before the police."

Evelyn looked down at the baby. "And discover who left this precious baby outside without a stitch of clothing to keep her warm."

"She will then return to the care of her parents." Tommy leaned forward. "You must prepare yourself for that eventuality. Please don't let yourself become so enraptured by her you forget she isn't yours to keep."

"Have you looked at her?" she asked. "I mean *really* looked at her. How could I fail to be completely besotted? She is so perfect."

"She's very sweet," he agreed. "But we will find her parents."

"Who are not suitable parents," Evelyn said vehemently. "If they were, they would not have left her on a doorstep."

"Where is the shawl she was wrapped in?"

"Mrs Chapman is arranging for it to be laundered."

As soon as Malton was aware there was a baby in the house, he had awakened the housekeeper. He was comfortable searching for a bassinet for the infant. As for the other paraphernalia required for a child, that was not something he had any knowledge of.

"I think that is our first clue in searching for the babe's parents."

"Can we not think of a name for her?" Evelyn shifted the baby to rest on her opposite arm. "Before you say it, Tommy, I know we can't keep her. A name would be temporary and just so we don't have to refer to her as 'the baby' all the time."

"Giving her a name is the very opposite of temporary. It implies a permanence we can't be certain of."

Evelyn's eyes gleamed with satisfaction. "You think the same as me, don't you?"

"Do I?" Tommy asked in defeat, for he already knew both her answer and his own.

"If her parents are inadequate, we should keep her."

Tommy nodded slowly. "If her parents cannot care for her, for whatever reason, we cannot allow her to go into the workhouse."

He couldn't bear to look at the exquisite joy on his wife's face. She would be beyond devastated if the child's parents could care for her after all.

"What about Perdita?"

"Lost?"

"I'd rather think of her as lost than abandoned."

"Would you?" he asked with surprise. "If she's lost, there's more chance of her parents returning for her."

"That would be better for her, wouldn't it? So that is what I shall hope for."

Malton opened the door. "Dr Michaels, My Lord."

Tommy got to his feet and crossed the room to greet the doctor. "Thank you for coming so promptly."

"You mentioned a baby found outside. I got here as quickly as I could." He reached out his arms toward Evelyn to take the infant.

She stood and passed the child over. It didn't matter if Dr Michaels was the type of doctor who liked to do his examinations in private, Tommy knew Evelyn would not leave the baby's side.

"What do you know about the circumstances of her birth?" the doctor asked as he removed the baby's clothing.

"Nothing, I'm afraid," Evelyn answered. "Are there police outside the front of the house?"

"Yes, My Lady. They are surely not guarding your house because of this foundling?"

"Unfortunately, a young man was found dead tonight. Perdita…the baby…was nearby."

"How unpleasant for you all," he murmured sympathetically. "Might the child belong to him? Or is he not known to you?"

"He knows my cousin," Tommy said. "We had not met him before this evening. There's no reason to believe the baby is his, but of course, we do not know him well enough to be certain of anything."

"I can confirm what you said on the telephone, Lord Northmoor. She is a healthy baby. So far as I can tell, she is of full term. As for when she was born, I can only give you an educated guess."

"What would you base that supposition on?" Evelyn asked, kneeling on the floor beside the doctor. She caught one of the child's flailing hands in her own.

One thing was certain, the baby did not like to be

undressed. Her screams bounced off the walls of the large room.

The doctor pointed to the exposed umbilical cord. "You see the colour of the stump? Following birth, it darkens as it dries out, and it eventually falls off a week or so later. She's most likely a couple of hours old, certainly no more than forty-eight hours at the extreme outer limit."

"That fits with what we know," Tommy said as he watched Evelyn re-dress Perdita. "We found her naked and wrapped in a shawl. My wife and our housekeeper bathed her and were certain, because of her condition, that the mother did not clean the child following her birth."

"I take it you will not require me to obtain a place for her at the workhouse?"

"Absolutely not." Evelyn looked up at him.

"As you can see," Tommy smiled indulgently at Evelyn. "My wife is very keen to care for the child herself. Luckily "

"I see that." The doctor nodded. "And the little mite already has a name. She is lucky to have been left on your doorstep. Most homes around here would have called for the police and had her removed immediately."

"The Lord calls on us to care for widows and orphans," he said a little self-consciously, then looked at the doctor. "I have spent a good deal of time with our village vicar back home. He's very outspoken on what he believes a person's obligations are. Especially a person such as me with the means to improve the existence of others."

John Capes, the man he referred to, was much more than a man of the church. Tommy classed him as a good friend. Although John based many of their discussions around Bible principles, Tommy found that most of their conversations had their basis in common sense and moral decency.

He had also helped to give Tommy some measure of peace following his difficulties in coming to terms with the things he had seen and done during the war.

"I'll arrange for a wet nurse to come over as soon as possible," Dr Michaels said. "Will you also require a nursemaid? I am certain my wife, or one of her friends, will know someone suitable."

"That would be extremely kind." Tommy shook the other man's hand. "We do have a couple of local staff who may know of someone. I think I can speak for Lady Northmoor as well as myself when I say we would both prefer to rely on your suggestions, given your experience."

Evelyn lifted the child onto her shoulder and patted her impossibly small back, whispering to her as she did so. Although it had been a shocking night, one thing had not surprised him, and that was that Evelyn had taken to caring for the baby as naturally as everything else she had done since he'd known her.

The doctor left, and Tommy moved over to her side. He wrapped his arms around Evelyn and kissed the top of her head. "I am incredibly proud of you, my darling."

She looked up at him in surprise. "What for?"

"Nothing, and everything," he responded. "Mostly just for being you."

CHAPTER 3

The door creaked open, and Victoria stood in the entrance to the library with an incredulous look on her face.

"Evelyn! My goodness…"

"Has the detective spoken to you?" Tommy asked.

"He's taken Lord Chesden off somewhere. He asked the rest of us to stay where we were, but I heard a baby crying and couldn't resist finding out more."

"How well did you know Georges Dubois?" Evelyn hoped her abrupt question would surprise Victoria into answering quickly. In her experience, a response given without too much thought was usually honest.

"Georges?" Victoria repeated and looked at Tommy, then back at Evelyn. She visibly gathered herself. The brief delay was long enough to give her time to decide how much she would share and which information she would keep to herself. "We knew Georges when we lived on the continent."

"He lived near you in France?"

"Why all the questions?" Victoria asked sharply, a note of suspicion in her voice.

"Didn't the detective say why he was here at the house?" Tommy interjected.

Victoria looked at her nephew. "He didn't. I presumed there had been a theft or something."

Evelyn frowned. "Why would that be your first impression?"

Victoria swept a hand around the room. "Houses like these attract the type of characters who would rather indulge in nefarious deeds than find gainful employment."

Evelyn hated generalisations. Especially when voiced by a woman who hadn't worked a day in her life. Still, she couldn't deny that it was a common opinion.

"I insist you tell me what is happening." Victoria stepped into the room and closed the door behind her. "Are you telling me there hasn't been a burglary?"

"I'm afraid it's much more serious than that." Evelyn sat in the chair next to the now blazing fire.

"Darling…" Tommy warned.

The police would not be pleased if she told Victoria what had happened to Georges. Still, if they had wanted the information to remain confidential until they had spoken to everyone in the drawing room, it was up to them to ensure that happened.

"Georges has been murdered," Evelyn said bluntly.

"But…" Victoria's gaze swung wildly to Tommy for confirmation. "But he was here earlier this evening and he was fine. You must be mistaken."

"Evelyn is telling the truth. We have both seen the body." Tommy moved over to the sideboard. "Would you like a drink, Aunt Victoria?"

"There is tea, if you would prefer." Evelyn lifted her own cup and took a sip.

"I don't want tea." Victoria shook her head. "Neither do I want sherry or anything else sweet and silly. Give me a measure of brandy, Tommy. And make it a large one."

Evelyn considered the older woman. She was acting shocked, as was to be expected. Victoria was saying the right things, but there was something missing. It would be normal for a person acquainted with a murder victim to ask what had happened and then make some sort of statement as to his character. Either he was the sort of person for whom murder wasn't a surprise or he was a pleasant young man, and his death was a terrible tragedy.

"Did you like Georges?"

"What a strange question." Victoria took the tumbler from Tommy and drank the liquid in one long swallow. "Fill it up, please."

Tommy lifted an eyebrow in Evelyn's direction as he walked back to the brandy decanter. Evelyn wasn't sure if it was because of her questions or the straightforward way Victoria had taken the measure of brandy with no discernible effect. If she herself drank that particular tipple, she coughed as it burned its way down her throat and then settled into a warm puddle in her stomach. She also pulled a face as if the drink was an extremely bitter medicine. If she hadn't watched Tommy pour the brandy for Victoria, she would've believed the glass contained liquid with no more potency than water.

Tommy replenished Victoria's drink and handed it over. "Tell us about Georges."

Victoria sighed, tired of being pressed over the dead man. "What do you want to know? He's just a penniless French boy who had a rather annoying tendency to follow Madeleine around."

"Aunt Victoria," Tommy said sternly. "Georges trailed your family all the way to England, and to this house. Now he's dead. Surely you must see how that will look to the police?"

She sat in the chair opposite Evelyn. "Now you've put it like that, I do see. They will jump to the conclusion I've done something to that silly boy."

"Did you?" Evelyn asked bluntly.

"How dare you!" Victoria's face flushed.

"I'm very tired." Evelyn looked at the grandfather clock in the corner of the room. "It is almost two in the morning. We left Yorkshire early *yesterday* morning to travel down to London to host your family. I think I deserve an answer."

Victoria looked at Tommy. "Are you going to let her talk to me like that?"

"Absolutely," Tommy said resolutely. "Lady Northmoor has kindly agreed to recommend Madeleine for presentation before the King. We have also gifted your family a substantial sum of money, to supplement the inheritance from your father, to ensure she has an adequate wardrobe. I apologise for my candid words, and have no wish to embarrass you, but I believe we deserve answers."

"I'm sorry." Victoria seemed to shrink in her seat. "Please forgive me. The shock has badly affected me."

Evelyn very much doubted that. More likely the timely reminder from Tommy that Victoria and her daughters were reliant on his good graces for not only a roof over their heads, but also if they wished to maintain even a pretence of decent social standing.

"I'm sure." Tommy took Victoria's empty glass, filled it once again, and returned it to her shaking hand. "Now, perhaps you can provide us some answers before the police take you for questioning?"

She nursed her drink, gazing at it as though it were a precious gem. "What do you want to know?"

"All about Madeleine and Georges. Did you know he would follow her here? Did you kill him? Why was this baby found near his body?"

"Did you pay him to leave England and go back to France?" Evelyn added.

"Goodness," Victoria laughed nervously, "such a lot of questions."

Tommy stared at her impassively. "I'm sure there will be more."

"I did not know Georges would come to England," Victoria began. "I fervently hoped he would not. Coming back to England was an attempt to prevent Madeleine from making a mistake with a penniless man like I did."

"Your marriage wasn't happy?" Evelyn couldn't imagine being tied to a man who made her unhappy.

"I was desperately in love with Louis. So much so that I ignored my father's warnings and ran away to be with him. He cut me off financially." She looked up. Her eyes reflected sadness. "I didn't understand what that would mean. Not really. I thought I did, but I was a silly girl of eighteen who didn't realise that passion and desire isn't at all the same as the lasting love one needs to make a marriage work."

Personally, Evelyn thought mutual respect went a long way to securing a successful marriage. She tried to recall what Aunt Em had told her about Victoria when Charles died, and the solicitor read his will to the family.

"You were married for many years." Evelyn had done some rough sums in her head. "I'm sorry it wasn't all you expected it would be."

Victoria shrugged and looked back at her drink. "Forty years of being married to a man who never stopped chasing other women despite how old he got, drowning his sorrows in a bottle, and blaming me for being cut off by my father. He thought marrying an earl's daughter would mean an endless supply of money."

Forty years of marriage, yet her eldest child was only twenty. Something did not add up. Evelyn wished she could think of some way of finding out, but that couldn't have anything to do with Georges's death, could it? She was so tired she could barely form a coherent thought, let alone a sentence.

"Did you kill him?" Tommy asked. "Maybe by accident because you wanted him to leave Madeleine alone?"

Victoria shook her head. "I admit I wanted him out of our lives, but I would never have killed him. I know what it is like to lose a child so I could not…"

The door opened and Detective Inspector Price stared angrily into the room. "What is going on here?"

"Aunt Victoria heard the baby crying," Tommy said. "She came to see where she'd come from."

"I suppose you expect me to believe you haven't been discussing the case?" He shook his head. "Don't bother answering. Mrs Bernard, I need you to come with me now, please."

Victoria got to her feet and paused by the side of Evelyn. She looked down at the baby. A loud gasp escaped her lips before she slapped a hand over her mouth.

"Gabrielle," she mumbled. "Oh, Gabrielle."

❧

*T*ommy accompanied Evelyn into the drawing room, as requested by the detective. He had positioned a uniformed officer outside the library, and Alexander and David Ryder waited inside that room to be questioned next.

"Where does one smoke around here, Northmoor?" Lord Chesden asked.

"Which room are the police using to question people?" Tommy asked.

"The dining room." He wrinkled his nose in distaste, then banged his cane on the floor. "I don't suppose you allow smoking in here?"

"No," Tommy answered. "And not in front of the ladies. Lady Chesden, have the police spoken to you?"

"Yes," she answered. "Directly after my husband. Not that I could tell them a thing of any importance."

"My wife will keep you company while I take your husband off so he can enjoy his cigar." Tommy walked toward the door. "Let's go to the ballroom."

"Terrific," Lord Chesden answered and followed Tommy.

His cane tapped loudly on the wooden floor in the hallway.

Tommy stopped at the door to the ballroom. "Can I ask Malton to get you a drink? He has a supply in his room."

"Bit late in the evening now, old man." The earl gave an embarrassed chuckle. "Shan't sleep if I drink anymore."

Tommy waited until they were settled in chairs and Fred was puffing away on a fat, pungent cigar. "I can't apologise enough. Jolly terrible thing to happen on our doorstep."

"Not your fault," Fred replied, then guffawed. "Well, unless you did it, of course. Then it would definitely be your fault."

"I can assure you it was nothing to do with me," Tommy said. "Never met the fellow before this evening."

"What would a French chap be doing in England?"

"Ah, the police told you where he was from. I wondered if they would."

"Apparently he is known to the Bernard family." Fred tipped back his head and blew smoke toward the ceiling. "Can't imagine they have anything to do with this. They're from a respectable family. Well, on the mother's side they are."

"You were friendly with my Uncle Charles, I believe?"

"He was a good man." Fred seemed to consider his words carefully. "Didn't know him awfully well. Our fathers were close, though. If things had been different, I would've married Victoria."

"Really?"

"Oh yes," Fred said confidently. "Our fathers arranged it. Well, actually, I was to marry Anne, but she died as a child.

Victoria was the next girl in line and our fathers agreed it would be a suitable match for our families."

Tommy thought back to the conversation he and Evelyn had just had with Victoria. She had chosen her husband and had not been happy. He couldn't imagine she would have been any more pleased by a marriage to Fred.

"What happened?"

He rather thought Louis Bernard was what had happened, but best to ask questions and let the older man talk. Who knew what he might find out? Especially after Victoria's strange reaction to the baby.

"Ran off with that French chap. He was an artist, if you can believe it. Her father was so furious Charles said he stopped her allowance and acted as though she was as dead as Anne."

"Was Edward angry because Victoria had run away before the arranged marriage, or because of the type of man Louis was?"

"Both I should imagine." Fred sucked noisily on his cigar. "It was the scandal of the year. And, of course, my father was livid your grandfather didn't have another daughter for me to marry."

"How terrible," Tommy muttered, wondering if Fred's father was cross because he didn't get the expected dowry into the family. "How did you feel about it?"

"I hadn't asked her to marry me. She hadn't been presented before she left with Louis. I easily found another woman who was suitable. My first wife was from a very prominent family. Not as wealthy as Sarah's though. Her family has an enormous estate in Ireland, you know."

"Really?" Tommy did his best to feign interest, but he didn't care at all who had the biggest estate, the most money, or the fanciest horses. He had always judged a person on how they treated him.

Fred Ryder didn't seem like a bad man. He was very

representative of the men of his era—distrusting of anyone who wasn't English, and who didn't adhere to strict social expectations.

"Had a rather decent few years as a single man between my first wife and Sarah." Fred winked.

Tommy wasn't sure of a decent response. He didn't know Fred very well and didn't talk about conquests, even with men he was friendly with. "How fortunate."

"I say." Fred coughed, cleared his throat, then pulled on his cigar again. "Where did that baby your wife have come from? I understood you and Lady Northmoor were childless?"

It was just a word. The other man had meant nothing by it. It was true he and Evelyn didn't have children yet. Childless seemed like such a permanent condition, and Tommy fought to keep his emotions under control. The excitement he had felt when Evelyn had told him she wanted to start a family with him had gradually faded as, month after month, she had failed to become pregnant.

"The baby was outside with the dead man."

"Ah, yes." Fred nodded. "I remember the detective telling me that. But why does your wife have the unfortunate creature in her arms?"

"We couldn't see the child go to the workhouse."

Fred frowned and stared uncomprehendingly at Tommy. "Why not? You don't know where it has come from. Its parents could be paupers."

"Whoever her parents are, it is not the baby's fault."

"Northmoor!" Fred shook his head sadly, as though Tommy had desperately disappointed him. "The child's mother is probably a common *streetwalker*."

"I suppose that is possible," Tommy conceded.

"And that doesn't bother you?"

"It would not stop us caring for the child," Tommy said firmly.

Fred stubbed out his cigar in a plant pot next to his chair and got to his feet. "Frankly, I am outraged."

"I am sorry you don't agree with our decision."

"It'll cause a terrible scandal." Fred walked a few steps toward the door, then gave up and flopped back into his chair. "I implore you to think of the young ladies and their reputations."

"Elise and Madeleine?" Tommy asked doubtfully. "No one would suggest the child belongs to one of them."

Fred waved a hand dismissively. "Of course not. They are respectable girls. I simply meant that the stain of having a child of uncertain parentage in the house may cause them problems when being presented in society."

Tommy was glad Fred used a polite way to describe the baby and not the word he was certain hovered on the tip of the other man's tongue. "Evelyn and I will bear your concerns in mind."

Fred looked like he would argue the matter further. He assessed Tommy through a fog of smoke. "May I speak plainly with you?"

Their discussions surely couldn't get much more honest. "Of course. Please do."

"Victoria wrote to me when she was planning to come back to England. At first, I thought she hoped to rekindle our personal relationship. However, she wanted to know about my sons. Alexander, in particular."

Of course she did. Victoria had left France in a hurry to get Madeleine away from Georges. There was no better way to make her daughter forget her French beau than to plunge her daughter into the social maelstrom that was the London Season. Why not help the girl along a little by ensuring there were a couple of eligible bachelors in the same house?

"She is interested in a match between Alexander and Madeleine?"

"We both favour such an arrangement."

Tommy leaned back in his chair. "I'm afraid her father died with no assets. Victoria has nothing but a small legacy from her father. There will be a small dowry that I will provide both girls with when the time comes."

Fred laughed in genuine amusement. "My sons may be chums with the Norton-Cavendish boy, but I can assure you our family does not suffer with the same financial issues."

"I'm glad to hear it." Tommy folded one leg over the other. "I hope Madeleine will find a husband who will cherish her for herself and not for family money they may hope she has."

"What a strange way to think." Fred shook his head. "Victoria married for love and look where that got her. It is much more satisfactory for marriage to be seen as a business transaction. Female emotions make things so much more difficult than they need to be."

Poor Lady Chesden.

"What about Elise? She is, after all, the elder sister."

"Ah, now this is a little awkward." Fred raised a hand and gave a delicate cough.

Tommy could hardly believe his ears. After the topics they had discussed, why was the man now affecting embarrassment?

"It's been an evening of revelations," Tommy said wearily. "You may as well tell me."

"I saw that young lady in a particularly compromising situation with Norton-Cavendish this evening. Victoria favoured Madeleine for Alexander and after what I saw, I must say that I wholeheartedly agree."

He had been right when he noticed Elise had left the drawing room, claiming a headache not long after Hugh. Was it now his responsibility to talk to Victoria about the information Fred had divulged? Tommy passed a hand across his tired face. Maybe after he had slept, things would make more sense.

~

*E*velyn shifted on the sofa and readjusted the position of the sleeping baby. Sarah Ryder looked over with interest but did not speak.

"I named her Perdita," Evelyn said to open up the conversation.

"Is that wise?" Sarah looked concerned. "The police said they will find the baby's parents. If you care for her personally, it will devastate you when she leaves. Best to get a girl in to care for her if you feel a responsibility for her because she was found here."

"Our doctor has visited and is arranging for both a wet nurse and a nursemaid."

Sarah looked relieved. "That is very sensible. After all, it would be very difficult to have such a child around when you and Lord Northmoor have your own children."

"Why?" Evelyn should probably have changed the subject to something less personal, especially because being tired was making her more emotional. Yet she wanted to know what the other woman thought. Sarah's opinion may well be indicative of popular opinion. What would people think of Evelyn taking in a child found on her doorstep?

"When you have children of your own, you will understand what I mean." Sarah pleated the skirt of her gown between her fingers. "You can love other children, of course. For example, I am very fond of my nieces and nephews. But there is no love like a mother has for her children. There is *nothing* I wouldn't do for my sons."

Evelyn filed that piece of information away for later. She couldn't imagine how the death of Georges could possibly have anything to do with any of the Ryder family.

However, she had often thought pieces of a puzzle couldn't possibly be linked to each other—right until the point they made sense. Experience had taught her that having all the pieces figuratively laid out in front of her was imperative.

She thought back to Victoria's face when she had looked at the baby. There was something very genuine in her reaction that had not been there when she had spoken about Georges's death.

Who was Gabrielle?

"The best outcome would be for Perdita's parents to be located and for the family to be reunited." Evelyn said the words and wished she meant them wholeheartedly. Of course, it would be best for the baby to be cared for by her mother. But if that were not possible, for whatever reason, she was more than ready to step in and take on a maternal role.

"Indeed." Sarah smoothed out the creases she'd made in her dress. "Did you know the poor young man who was murdered?"

Evelyn recognised the woman's casual question for what it was. Sarah Ryder was trying to find out what Evelyn knew. She didn't know what the police had said. Had they told Sarah that Georges was at the house looking for Madeleine? When he had burst into the drawing room, Sarah was still upstairs.

"I am told he was French," Evelyn said vaguely.

"Perhaps it is coincidental that Lady Victoria and her daughters have so recently returned from France."

"I met Aunt Victoria, Elise, and Madeleine for the first time yesterday." Evelyn deliberately avoided commenting on Sarah's insinuation that it seemed unlikely the family did not know Georges.

"My husband is rather keen on our eldest son, Alexander, making a match with Madeleine. From what I have seen during our brief acquaintance, Madeleine would be much more suited to my younger son, David."

Sarah's entire countenance altered when she spoke about

her youngest. Evelyn couldn't help but wonder if the woman's sons were aware of her very obvious favouritism.

"How so?"

"Madeleine is a quiet girl and dresses modestly, as a young woman should. Elise, on the other hand, is somewhat outspoken and as you saw this evening favours the type of gown popular on the continent." Sarah wrinkled her nose in distaste. "Thin, inadequate material and a neckline that was most indecent."

Evelyn tried to think back to how the two girls presented at dinner. Madeleine was quiet and demure, that was true. However, Elise had not seemed particularly talkative either. She had thought the girl's dress rather pretty. Dove grey with sequins was a combination Evelyn herself would wear. Sarah had a point regarding the neckline. Personally, she would not feel comfortable with quite so much flesh showing.

In contrast, Madeleine wore a drop-waisted dress that was more popular in England and was certainly more suitable for a young girl waiting to be presented at court.

"How do Alexander and David differ in personalities?"

Sarah smiled, seeming pleased to talk about her boys. "Alexander is more like his father. Of course, he works closely with him as one day he will inherit, so it is understandable they are more alike."

"What does David do?"

"David is a lawyer." Pride radiated from Sarah as she spoke about her younger son. "Madeleine would make him a very nice wife. A perfect solicitor's wife. Her dress was understated, she spoke intelligently when spoken to, and was very modest in her ways. I particularly noticed that while her sister was happy to expose too much skin, Madeleine carried a shawl to maintain her dignity."

A vision of Madeleine in the drawing room when she caught sight of Georges flittered through Evelyn's mind. The girl was standing near the door with a small clutch bag in one hand and a shawl draped over her arm. She held her hands in front of her body, which certainly supported Sarah's claims of the girl's high level of decorum.

"Such a pretty shawl," Evelyn murmured as though it was of no consequence. "Do you remember what colour it was?"

Sarah thought for a moment. "It was pink, I believe. A very pale pink."

The shawl covering Perdita in the basket was a deep red. There could be no suggestion that it was the same item. Though, Evelyn realised, a lady would have many shawls of different colours in her wardrobe. It was important that she get the article back from Mrs Chapman as soon as it was clean so she could ask the female guests if they had one like it.

"If you will excuse me, Lady Northmoor, I think I will see if my husband has finished smoking and is ready to retire." Sarah stood and moved over to look at the baby. "I can see why you can't stop staring at her. She's an extraordinarily beautiful child."

"May I ask you one last thing before you leave?"

"Of course."

"Do you have any idea who she may belong to, or why she was left on our kitchen doorstep?"

"I most certainly do not," Sarah said stridently. "What a peculiar question."

"Thank you," Evelyn sighed as she looked down at Perdita. What a terrible evening it had been. "Good night."

CHAPTER 4

The uniformed officer was so flummoxed at being spoken to by an earl that it was easy for Tommy to convince him to let him into the library on the pretence of getting a drink.

Fred and Sarah Ryder had retired to their room. Tommy longed to climb the stairs himself and sink into a deep sleep. It had been some years since he had been as tired as he was at that present moment.

As he slipped into the room, it was apparent he had interrupted a heated discussion between the brothers.

"Northmoor," Alexander said with no attempt to hide his irritation.

In contrast, his brother smiled politely. "Good evening, Lord Northmoor. Dashed awful business this."

"Dreadful," Tommy agreed. "Hopefully the police will be finished with you soon and you can get to bed."

"My brother would rather stay up and greet Miss Bernard when she comes down for breakfast," Alexander drawled.

"Is that right?" Tommy turned to David and smiled. "Which of my cousins has captured your attention?"

"It does not matter which sister either of us likes."

Alexander tipped back his head and swallowed the last dregs of his drink.

He set the glass down heavily on a nearby table, telling Tommy that he had consumed rather too much liquor for one night. His jacket was slung carelessly over the back of a chair, his tie loosened, and his hair no longer neatly slicked down as it had been when he'd finally come down for dinner.

His conversation with Fred Ryder had prepared him for this conversation, and so Tommy already understood the reason for Alexander's frustration. "I understand your father is keen on securing a match between you and Madeleine."

"And what Father wants, he will get. I wouldn't be surprised if one morning Mother fails to wake up because he's done away with her so he can finally marry Lady Victoria."

"Now, Alex." David reached out a hand to pat his brother's arm. "Let us not talk hastily. Especially on an evening when a murder has already occurred. Please watch what you say when you speak to the police."

"I'm surprised you know about your father's previous friendship with my aunt," Tommy said carefully.

"I don't think it's a secret." Alexander smirked. "Few things are in London. I don't suppose you'd know much about that. You usually stay on your estate, don't you? I can't think what you do all day long up there. It must be so boring."

Tommy thought about the recent cases he and Evelyn had solved. Hessleham was a long way from boring. On the surface, it was a little country village like so many all over the country. However, underneath, it was boiling with as much passion, repressed emotions, and machinations as London.

"You would be surprised," Tommy said mildly.

"I say." David turned to Tommy. "Wasn't your uncle murdered last year?"

"That's right." Tommy watched Alexander's face carefully

as he spoke his next words. "Poisoned by the brandy he habitually drank each evening before dinner."

"Then you inherited his title?" Alexander sneered, but his voice lacked its previous self-assurance.

"Not quite." Tommy pulled a face. "Someone went on to shoot my cousin Eddie after his father was killed. I inherited the title at that time."

"Wasn't that a little convenient for you?"

"Not really." Tommy held out his hands, palms up. "I never had a desire to become Lord Northmoor. In fact, there are still days when I wish I could pass the title and its accompanying responsibilities on to my brother. Even if that were possible, it wouldn't be advisable. Harry is only nineteen."

"Had this dead French fellow been poisoned?" Alexander stared at his empty tumbler.

"I don't believe so." Tommy was certain poor Georges had received a deadly stab wound, but it was for the home officer pathologist to determine the cause of death.

"Does that mean you're not a suspect?"

"Not this time," Tommy confirmed. "At least, not so far as I know."

"Were you suspected of your uncle's death?" David asked.

"They actually arrested me for it," Tommy admitted. "That is what led Evelyn and I to investigate the murder. So we could clear my name. Before the war, I worked in the police force, so I had some experience in conducting an enquiry. Evelyn and I were able to uncover the murderer's identity."

"Your *wife*?"

"You shouldn't underestimate Evelyn simply because she is a woman."

"I'm afraid my brother thinks women have only one use," David scoffed. "That is what we were discussing when you came in."

Tommy chuckled to hide his anger. "How dangerous."

"I was simply commenting on what an attractive girl Elise is," Alexander said defensively.

"Yet your father thinks you should pay attention to Madeleine?"

Alexander used the arm rests on the chair to lever himself upright. Grabbing his empty glass, he went over to the decanter and poured himself a drink. Without offering to get a drink for either his brother or Tommy, he returned to his seat.

"Let's get one thing clear, Northmoor." Alexander swirled the liquid around and stared at it morosely. "He doesn't want me to talk to the girl at social functions and ask her for a couple of dances. Father fully expects me to propose by the end of the summer."

David stared resolutely ahead, as though his brother's words had no effect on him whatsoever.

"Is that what you want?"

Alexander's head snapped up and his eyes blazed with frustration. "I've told you. It doesn't matter what we want. Father is the Earl of Chesden. Not only does that usually guarantee him his own way, but he controls the allowance I receive."

"Father has offered Alex a rather colossal sum of money if he marries Madeleine before Christmas."

"Are my cousin's wishes to be considered at all in this matter?"

"Not by Father." Alexander shook his head. "It's common knowledge that side of your family is disadvantaged, from an economic standpoint. I expect he believes he can buy what he wants. He usually does."

"I can't believe Aunt Victoria would agree to this."

"Come on now," Alexander said. "You cannot be that naïve. People will do almost anything for money."

He knew arrangements happened between families, but he'd never really stopped to consider how many of the brides and grooms were marrying completely voluntarily. What a terrible way to treat your children—as though they were of no more importance than animals bought and sold at market.

Elise and Madeleine may not be his children, but he determined right then neither of his cousins would marry any man unless it was their choice. He must speak directly to Victoria in the morning to find out the level of her complicity in Fred Ryder's plans.

~

*E*velyn rested her chin on one upturned hand. Her elbow sat on the kitchen table and was the only thing stopping her from toppling onto the stone floor.

"Why don't you go to bed, My Lady?" Mrs O'Connell, the cook, asked. "Doris has already gone up."

"How strange to talk about going to bed at six in the morning." Evelyn sipped the sweet tea the cook had placed on the table next to her.

"It's been an odd twenty-four hours from what I can tell. You should have had Doris or Mrs Chapman wake me, My Lady."

"We didn't all need to be up." Evelyn yawned. "The baby slept after we bathed her. I expect she was exhausted from her arrival into the world."

"At least help has arrived now." Mrs O'Connell eyed Evelyn. "Will you keep her?"

It was a conversation she would have to have properly with Tommy. Neither of them wanted Perdita to end up in the workhouse, but was it right to take her to Yorkshire and raise her as their own child when she likely had family here in London?

"The wet nurse has agreed to work for us until the baby is weaned. The nursemaid will stay with us as long as we remain in London. She doesn't want to come to Yorkshire when we return."

"Are they responsible staff?" Mrs O'Connell wondered. She looked around before continuing. "The staff here are adequate, but nothing like those we have at Hessleham Hall."

Evelyn smiled. "Are you missing Nora?"

Nora was the kitchen assistant and had stayed home to cook for the staff who had remained at the manor. Their home in Belgrave Square usually had only a skeleton staff, as the family didn't tend to use it very often. They employed temporary help when Victoria asked to stay, but Evelyn wanted to bring their most senior and trusted staff with them. At least they would ensure they ran the household to her and Tommy's liking.

"I am, My Lady. She often knows what I want in the kitchen before I know myself."

"You're very close to her, are you not?"

Mrs O'Connell fussed with the table, running a cloth over it even though it was already spotless. "She's a nice enough young lass, even if she never stops chattering on."

Evelyn smothered a grin. That was high praise enough from Mrs O'Connell. Goodness knew what would happen if the butcher's boy from the village got himself together and proposed to Nora. Eventually Nora would leave her post and poor Cook would be lost without her, and she knew it.

"Tell me what happened last night," Evelyn said. "From the time Madeleine brought Georges down to the kitchen."

Mrs O'Connell frowned as she tried to recall the details. "She said Lord Northmoor had arranged for Georges to eat with you, but he refused. She asked if he could eat with us. I said if that was alright with you then that is what we would do."

"And did he stay down here and have his meal?"

"He did," Mrs O'Connell confirmed. "Not that we really

knew he was here. Didn't say anything other than to thank me for the food."

"Then what did he do?"

"Frank Douglas, the footman, said he saw him on the stairs."

"What was he doing?"

"Frank said he was standing at the top of the servants' stairs. He says the French boy looked like he was waiting for someone."

Evelyn frowned. "I don't suppose Frank asked him who he was waiting for?"

Mrs O'Connell shook her head. "Said he noticed him as he was up and down with the food, but he didn't speak to him."

"You and Lord Northmoor aren't really going to do your sleuthing here in London, are you? Especially now you've got that bairn to look after?"

"If not us, then who?"

"Begging your pardon, My Lady, but the police. It is them who get paid for that type of work after all."

Evelyn waved a dismissive hand. "You know how this works, Mrs O'Connell. Lots of people will not talk to the police. They will, however, talk to us. Sometimes because they are intimidated by Tommy and his title. Usually though, because people see us as harmless."

"I remember last time you almost had the life choked out of you, My Lady. I'm shocked His Lordship hasn't banned you from becoming involved."

"Do you really see Lord Northmoor banning me from doing something?" Evelyn raised an eyebrow.

Mrs O'Connell made a noise that was somewhere in between a snort and a laugh. "I do not."

"I promise to be very careful."

Mrs O'Connell turned to the stove and stirred something. "I'm sure, My Lady."

The cook had a habit of blustering her way through something she found emotionally challenging. She would do whatever she could to make sure they did not see her feelings. Which actually had the opposite effect. Everyone knew that if Mrs O'Connell had her back to people whilst they were talking about something difficult, she was more than likely wiping away a tear or at the very least composing herself.

"Now, might you know someone named Gabrielle?"

"Gabrielle, My Lady?"

"This girl may be a woman now." Evelyn shrugged. "I don't know what I mean, really. I'm so tired. Lady Victoria mentioned that name when she looked at the lost child. Did you work at Hessleham Hall when Victoria lived there?"

"I was nothing but a scullery maid back then," Mrs O'Connell's eyes focussed on the wall behind Evelyn. She had a slight smile on her lips, as though recalling something pleasant. "Was this Gabrielle connected to Lady Victoria?"

"I think she must have been. Could there have been a sister, or a niece? Some kind of close relation like that?"

"I don't remember a Gabrielle. Lady Emily would be the best person to answer that. There's nothing she doesn't remember about the family tree."

"Of course. How silly of me. Lady Victoria wrote to Lady Emily for years while she lived in France. I shall speak to her."

"My Lady," said the cook, "if you don't mind my saying, it would be best if you were to lie down and sleep for at least a few hours. Maybe when you are rested, sleuthing will be a little easier?"

"Mrs O'Connell, I don't mind you saying so. Of course, you are quite right." Evelyn wearily got to her feet. "Perhaps you would ask Mrs Chapman to wake me mid-morning? There are so many things I must do."

"I will, My Lady, but mind you don't go wearing yourself out."

It was excellent advice, but Evelyn didn't see herself

taking it until she and Tommy had solved the murder of Georges and worked out who baby Perdita belonged to.

~

*D*etective Inspector Price asked to speak to Evelyn and Tommy before they went to their room.

"I've sent Ada out to the shops to buy whatever she thinks Perdita needs for the next few weeks," Evelyn told Tommy.

"Who is Ada?" Tommy couldn't keep up with the changes in the household, though, in fairness, he was so tired he would struggle to remember his own name if asked.

"The nursemaid we employed based on the recommendation of Dr Michaels."

"Nursemaid, right." Tommy opened the door to the library. "I'll try to remember that."

They entered the room and sat together on the sofa. The detective got up from his chair near the window and walked over to stand in front of them.

"This is my investigation and I expect you both to respect that," he said, his voice firm. "Is that understood?"

"Of course." Tommy crossed one ankle over the other and rolled his shoulders. "Was there something you particularly wanted to discuss with us? My wife is incredibly tired. She also has undertaken caring for an infant she has taken responsibility for so needs her rest."

"We still have Lady Emily Christie and Elise and Madeleine Bernard to speak to." The detective looked at his notes. "At that point we will leave the house under the guard of a team of four uniformed officers. We will post one at each entrance to the house. The other two will be inside the house where their duty is primarily to keep everyone safe while we, Harrington and I, investigate and follow up enquiries."

"You think someone from inside our home committed the murder?"

The detective raised a surprised eyebrow. "Don't you?"

"Indeed I do," Tommy said regretfully. "Is there anything else you can tell us about what happened to Georges?"

"It appears that a long, thin-bladed weapon killed him. There will be a full examination, but that's the initial opinion of the Home Office pathologist. That is the primary purpose of my discussion at this time. Is there such an implement in the house?"

"Why do you believe someone from within this house committed the murder?" Evelyn asked.

Her question gave Tommy time to think through each room and whether it might contain a weapon such as the one Price suggested was used to kill Georges.

"It's very difficult to access your courtyard from the back of the house," the detective explained. "I had Harrington here try to do it."

"How clever," Evelyn murmured.

"He finally gained access after several attempts. Getting out of the courtyard proved more difficult."

"How so?" she asked. "Surely he just needed to unlatch the gate and walk through?"

"If we are to believe everyone, that gate wasn't just latched shut. It was also bolted. Your cook…" He flipped through his notebook. "Mrs O'Connell states she knows they definitely pushed home the bolt. She checks this herself before she retires for the night."

"That sounds like Mrs O'Connell." Evelyn leaned forward in her chair. "She is a very loyal and thorough member of staff. Her word can certainly be trusted."

"The murderer therefore did not escape out into the back streets, but back into the house. Unfortunately, there had been much activity in the kitchen between us learning that information and examining the kitchen thoroughly."

"It is only to be expected you assumed the murderer had

escaped through the gate," Evelyn said soothingly. "Were you able to find anything in the kitchen?"

"There appeared to be a slight trace of blood on a tap." The detective shrugged. "It wasn't a big enough spot for us to be certain it was even blood. Furthermore, kitchen staff admitted to using that sink on numerous occasions this morning."

"The conclusion is that someone killed Georges, washed his hands in the kitchen sink, then went back upstairs as though nothing had happened?"

"That is our theory." The detective inclined his head. "Most of your guests remained downstairs after dinner. They can alibi each other. Three guests retired early. We will question them when they arise."

"Those are your only suspects?" Tommy asked.

"Those are our major suspects," the detective corrected. "We will rule no one out. In my considerable experience, people tend to lie to the police. Particularly those who have something to hide."

Tommy bristled at the man's supercilious tone. He breathed deeply through his nose. It wouldn't do for him to lose his temper with the detective. If he were to do so, they might not continue to share information with him.

"Could the weapon be an ice pick?" Evelyn offered the suggestion. "Malton, our butler, would be the best person to ask about that."

"I keep a letter opener on the desk over there." Tommy pointed to the corner of the room.

Price strode over and looked at the surface of the imposing mahogany desk. He beckoned to Tommy. "Come over here and show me where it usually is."

Tommy walked over, his heart hammering. He knew the evidence pointed to the murderer being a family member of one of his guests, but he didn't want to face it.

He pointed to the right-hand side of the desk. "It is always there, at the bottom corner."

The detective bent and looked underneath the desk. Standing up, he looked at Tommy. "It appears to be missing."

Tommy moved over to stand next to the detective. He swept his eyes over the desk in a vain hope he would see something the other man had missed.

Eventually he shook his head in defeat. "It's not here. It is very distinctive. Silver with a Scottish basket hilt."

"Sharp enough to kill?"

"I'm afraid so."

"Harrington, get on the telephone and let the station know we need more uniformed officers. This entire house needs searching immediately. We find the weapon, we've found our murderer."

"ind the weapon, we've found the murderer," Evelyn mocked. "Surely a detective with his *experience* knows that isn't how it works."

"Calm down, darling. Come and lie down." Tommy patted the bed next to him. "We've been up all night."

She was in no mood to be placated. "Aren't you furious?"

"The man is a fool," Tommy replied. "He irritates me, but that only makes me more determined to find the murderer before he does."

"Right, then let's do exactly that." Evelyn sat down on the edge of the bed. "What do we know?"

"Georges was involved with Madeleine. Or, at the least, he wanted to be."

"They were definitely involved," Evelyn said with certainty. "Georges didn't come over to England then happen to find the address where Madeleine was staying. She had to have told him."

"There are several people in the house who did not want Georges around and would be only too pleased that he is now out of the picture. Shall we go through them?"

"Your Aunt Victoria is the most likely suspect, I'm afraid. Let's start with her."

Tommy grimaced. "She does rather seem to have the best motive, doesn't she? Okay, so Victoria wants better for Madeleine than a penniless Frenchman. She favours a union between Madeleine and Alexander Ryder."

"Do we think she wants that because she has unrequited feelings for Fred and she wants to stay close to him, because of the social prestige that marriage would bring her, or completely altruistically because Madeleine will be financially secure and one day have a title of her own?"

"I wish I could say honestly it is the latter," Tommy replied honestly. "But I'm really not certain. I don't know her character enough to judge her intentions."

"I don't think Aunt Em could help with that. Although she says she and Victoria were close, that was years ago. The teenaged girl Victoria was before she ran off to France and the mature woman she is now are two completely different people."

"I agree." He reached out and rested a hand on her thigh. "What about Fred?"

Evelyn put a hand over Tommy's. This far into their marriage, they were attuned to each other's emotions. The very simple contact he offered was exactly what she needed. "I know he wants Alexander and Madeleine to marry, just as Victoria does. But is such an idea realistic? Things are very different now than they were when Victoria and Fred were young adults."

"Is it something you would kill over?" Tommy mused. "It seems rather extreme."

"I suppose that goes for his wife, too. She favours the younger son, David, but again, how likely is it she would kill a man just to give her son a chance of marrying a woman he's known for little more than a week?"

"I wish we could've been here earlier to see how everyone

interacted with each other before we arrived. We've missed things that could be crucial to the relationships between everyone."

"We can't change that now," Evelyn said pragmatically. "What about Alexander and David?"

"Alexander is certainly enough like his father for me to believe he is capable of murder. However, both brothers were clear that Alexander's interest is in Elise, despite his father's manoeuvrings behind the scenes. He has no motive."

"Based on that reasoning, we agree that David does?"

Tommy nodded. "He seems like a decent chap, but we know that appearances are deceptive when it comes to murder. We can't dismiss him from our enquiries simply because I rather like him."

"The others we don't know enough about to judge. We know they all had reasons for leaving the drawing room soon after dinner. Madeleine said she had invites to answer, Hugh said he hadn't slept well the night before and was tired, and Elise claimed to have a headache."

"They don't have alibis," Tommy said. "We need to question the others. Were the five of them together all evening, or did someone leave for any reason?"

Evelyn patted Tommy's hand. "We also must find out more about who Gabrielle is. I asked Mrs O'Connell, but she didn't know."

"Shall we sleep for a few hours now that we've talked that through?" Tommy took hold of Evelyn's hand and drew her closer to him.

She nodded, moved up the bed and slipped under the covers next to Tommy. She rested her head on his chest, their hands still clasped together. "Thank you for not haranguing me about Perdita."

Tommy rubbed his thumb over her knuckles. "I have already told you I am worried about you, and why. We succeed together, and we fail together. We gain as one, and we lose as one. Your pain is my pain, Evelyn. Whatever happens we will bear it together."

He kissed the top of her head and she thanked God for sending her a husband like Tommy.

❧

Tommy's first impression of Hugh Norton-Cavendish had been that he was a pleasant-looking young man, but hopelessly overshadowed by Alexander and David Ryder. Hugh had fair hair, was of average height, with even features. It was incomprehensible to Tommy that a flamboyant young woman like Elise would be interested in a nondescript fellow like Hugh when he kept company with the Ryder brothers.

He shut the library door and sat in the chair opposite Hugh. The young man closed the book he was reading and looked expectantly at Tommy.

"Can I help you, Lord Northmoor?"

Hugh spoke in a well-modulated voice. He displayed none of the open arrogance of Alexander or the quiet integrity of David. "I wanted to see how you were. I know you arrived here a week or so before my wife and I. Now we are in residence, and particularly after the events of last night, I wanted to see if there was anything we could do to make your stay more comfortable."

"I can't believe that poor young fellow was murdered."

"It has been rather a shock."

"I understand he was involved with Madeleine?"

Tommy wasn't sure how to answer the question. While he believed that was accurate, he wasn't sure that his Aunt Victoria or Madeline for that matter, would want that knowledge widely known. "I'm afraid I don't really keep up with family gossip."

If Hugh was surprised at Tommy's reluctance to answer

the question, he did not say so, nor did it show on his face. "Are the police still here?"

"The detectives have left. However, there's a uniformed police officer at the main entrance and another at the door at the back of the house leading to the kitchen. They also said two officers would be stationed inside the house to ensure everyone's safety until they complete their investigation."

Hugh held up his book. "I came straight in here to read after breakfast. Perhaps that's why I haven't seen anyone."

"You retired early last night." Tommy studied Hugh's face while he spoke. "I hope you slept well as I understand you had trouble the night before."

Hugh laughed a little nervously. "I am one of those people that struggles to get to sleep in new surroundings."

Did that mean he had slept well or not? Tommy was none the wiser. He had wanted to know whether Hugh was claiming to have slept all night or whether it was possible he had got out of bed and committed murder. "Had you ever met Georges?"

"Not to my knowledge."

Tommy decided to shift the conversation. "Until yesterday, I do hope you have been enjoying your stay. I understand you have been friends with Alexander and David since school?"

Hugh let out a pent-up breath and his shoulders lost some of their stiffness. "Yes, the three of us have always been good chums. It was very kind of you to extend their invitation to include me."

"I hadn't met Lord Chesden before yesterday, but his family and ours have enjoyed a long acquaintance." It was one of the things he disliked most about his new position as Lord Northmoor. He was expected to invite, and accept invitations, from people he had never met simply because generations of particular families had been close. "You are here for the Season? I attended a couple myself years ago. I must admit, I found some of the social events quite excruciating, though I'm certain they are much worse for the ladies than for us chaps."

"Yes, I am an only child, and my father is putting considerable pressure on me to marry and produce an heir. I'm sure you know how that is."

He did. Before being Lord Northmoor, Tommy had lived his life without a single thought about children other than knowing one day he would quite like to be a father. Although there was no family patriarch to increase the burden on him, he felt it all the same.

"Is there a young lady who has already caught your attention? Or are you hoping to meet someone during the forthcoming events?" Tommy didn't want to ask Hugh outright about what Lord Chesden claimed to have seen.

"There is someone who I am very fond of." Hugh looked down at his book. "It seems rather crass to speak of emotion and money in the same sentence. But the truth is, marrying someone as poor as myself would not do my family any good."

The other man's honesty surprised Tommy. It was not common for someone to admit their family was struggling financially. Of course, Tommy had heard the rumours about Hugh's father and his penchant for outlandish bets on the horses. "I'm terribly sorry to hear that."

"Life doesn't always happen the way we want it to, does it, Lord Northmoor?"

"Rarely," Tommy said. "In my experience, we spend our lives reacting to things that happen to us, rather than being able to choose our path and follow it without deviation."

Hugh nodded. "You did not expect to inherit your title, I understand?"

"Absolutely not," Tommy replied with a chuckle. "My cousin, Eddie, was in line to inherit from his father Charles. When I was born, there was an uncle and another cousin who would have inherited before me. Unfortunately, they were both killed during different military action. Last summer, the death of my uncle and cousin catapulted me into a position I was not prepared for, and did not expect."

"Have you now adjusted to your position?"

As much as Tommy was enjoying his talk with Hugh, who was refreshingly sincere, he wasn't finding out anything about where Hugh had been the previous evening or with whom. "I think I am still a work in progress. I have very good staff and feel secure leaving the estate in their capable hands while I am down here in London. However, truthfully, city life is not for me. Once we have finished hosting Lady Victoria and her daughters, Evelyn and I will be glad to go back to Yorkshire."

"Lady Victoria told us at dinner the other evening that Lady Northmoor is presenting her youngest daughter, Madeleine, at court."

Tommy smiled, as he often did when thinking about his wife. "Evelyn thought a change of scenery would be good for both of us. We agreed to host my aunt and cousins as we had been involved in a couple of unfortunate situations at home. We both believed London would be a pleasant escape from what had happened. Unfortunately, it seems that murder has followed us south."

"What do you mean?"

"Evelyn and I solved Uncle Charles's and Cousin Edward's murders. Our local member of Parliament was then killed on the grounds of our home. Evelyn and I found the perpetrator of that offence as well. Most recently, a rather unsavoury fellow was killed outside the village church. Evelyn cleverly ascertained who the offender was on that occasion."

"How terrible."

Tommy folded his hands in his lap. Chatting about mundane matters would not get him the answers he needed.

"I apologise if this question seems a little forward. However, as I have just said, we have had some success in uncovering people with nefarious intent. Were you in your room last night? That is to say, when you retired to bed after dinner, did you stay in your room all night without leaving?"

Hugh flushed and looked away. "I was."

Tommy hoped Hugh did not make a habit of playing cards. He was a terrible liar. "I'm sure the police have already asked you that question. May I suggest you practice your delivery? They are bound to speak to you again and you should really work on your answer if you want them to believe you."

~

*E*velyn held the baby protectively against her body as she walked into the drawing room. She had not seen Aunt Em since she had taken responsibility for Perdita. The opinion of Tommy's great-aunt mattered greatly to Evelyn. She had slept for a couple of hours before Mrs Chapman woke her, as previously arranged. Evelyn went straight to talk to the nursemaid and check on the baby.

"Goodness, Evelyn, there you are at last!" Aunt Em patted the seat next to her. "Sit next to me, dear."

Evelyn smiled and allowed herself to relax slightly. "Good afternoon, Aunt Em, Elise."

"Who do we have here?" Aunt Em asked.

Evelyn looked at Elise as she answered. "This is the baby that was found next to Georges's body last night. I have named her Perdita."

Aunt Em leaned over to look at the baby. "What a beautiful child. And a very apt name. She is indeed lost, isn't she?"

"I'm afraid so. It's incredibly sad. I am hopeful the police will be able to uncover the identity of her parents during their enquiries." Elise did not get up to look at the child, nor did she ask questions. She looked on the verge of tears. "Where is Madeleine?"

"Unwell." Elise looked at Evelyn when she spoke, but quickly glanced away.

"I must be mistaken," Evelyn said. "I thought it was you who suffered from a headache last night."

"That is correct."

"How very unfortunate you were unwell last night, and your sister is suffering today."

"The infernal tap tap tap of Lord Chesden's cane is enough to give anyone a headache," Aunt Em commented. "And if that doesn't do it, his overbearing conversational manner will certainly do it."

Elise gave Em a grateful look. "That is possibly what it was."

"Is Madeleine well enough to take her meals downstairs?" Evelyn asked. "Or should I arrange for the staff to serve her meals in her room?"

"I think Mother would prefer Madeleine to come down," Elise said. "She can be rather forceful if she deems it necessary."

Evelyn had no problems believing that if Victoria wanted something to happen, it would occur. She had packed up her entire life in France and moved her girls to England to avoid a man she thought not good enough to court her youngest daughter.

"How well did you know Georges?"

Elise threw a nervous look at the closed door of the drawing room. "Much better than my mother suspects."

"He was fond of your sister?"

"They were in love." Elise's bottom lip quivered. "Mother was outraged when she found out. She would have done anything to prevent Georges and Madeleine from continuing their relationship."

Aunt Em looked at her great-niece. "Anything? It might be a good idea if you did not say that to the police."

"Even if it is true?" Elise's expression turned sulky. "Because I believe there isn't a thing she wouldn't do to make sure Madeleine marries a very rich man. Preferably Alexander Ryder."

"Why him?" Evelyn wondered out loud as she stared down at the precious bundle she held in her arms.

Elise lifted a slim shoulder. "He is from a prominent family, he has a title, and is wealthy. I don't think it would matter to Mother whether he was attractive or repulsive, so I suppose Madeleine is jolly lucky that he happens to be a nice-looking fellow."

"Are you upset that your mother is focusing on finding a husband for Madeleine, but not for you?" Aunt Em asked. "You are the elder sister, after all."

"If Mother is busy concentrating on Madeleine, it means I can do what I like. That suits me fine."

Evelyn understood that. Her own mother had not been very attentive to either her needs or those of Evelyn's older sister, Milly. While that was sometimes upsetting, it also meant their adolescent years were a lot less restrictive than those of their peers. The only time Evelyn could remember having to toe the line was when she had come down to London and stayed with her father's sister for her own debut Season.

"Do you have a beau?"

Elise fiddled with the gold cord that ran down the outer section of the chair arm. "No."

"Oh, do come on now," Aunt Em said. "There must be a young man that has caught your notice. Or have you not yet been out much since you arrived?"

"I would prefer to take my time before deciding on one particular chap."

"That's very sensible." Evelyn couldn't help thinking that,

despite Elise's words, there was already somebody that she was fond of. It was clear in her demeanour and reluctance to look at either Evelyn or Em. "Can you tell us more about Georges?"

Elise looked relieved that conversation had moved on from her own private life. "What would you like to know?"

"You said earlier that you knew Georges far better than your mother believed. What did you mean by that?"

"Georges has been sweet on Madeleine for well over a year. I suppose I should say 'had been.' That sounds so very strange. Last night he was alive, here in London, and hoping to rekindle his romance with Madeleine. Now he's dead."

Evelyn leaned forward and passed Elise a handkerchief. "I'm so very sorry to have caused you distress."

"Aunt Em told me you and Tommy have had success in the past in solving several murder cases." Elise dried the tears from her face. "I don't mind your questions upsetting me if that helps you find whoever killed Georges."

"Your mother didn't approve of Georges because he was poor. Do you think that was the real reason?"

"That was the *only* reason. You do not know how awful our life was when Father was alive. We had very little money, though Mother always had enough to replenish her supply of gin."

Evelyn thought Victoria was fond of a drink. No, that wasn't quite true. She and Aunt Em enjoyed an evening gin and tonic, but it was her opinion Victoria *needed* the alcohol.

"I'm not sure I understand what you're saying," Evelyn said. "I hear what you say about your mother's drinking. How does that connect to Georges and his lack of funds?"

"Father only had money when he sold a painting. He only painted when he was in love. We all knew when Father had a new female friend because his output was incredible. The more he painted, the more Mother drank. He could always sell his paintings for very reasonable sums. We were happy then." Elise stared into the low fire. "We had new things, our parents were happy together again, Mother drank less. But there would always be another woman."

"I'm so very sorry, my dear," Aunt Em murmured. "I have kept up a correspondence with your mother for years, but I never suspected that is how you all lived. Her letters were full of how wonderful life in France was, how she had remained passionately in love with your father, and how successful he was as an artist."

"Father could have been world-renowned. I'm not just saying that. He was extremely talented. Unfortunately, he just did not have the drive needed to be successful unless he was in the first throes of love."

"Could your mother have killed Georges?" Evelyn asked gently.

"Oh, most definitely," Elise answered immediately. "She didn't want either Madeleine or me to live the life she led in France. That is, she wouldn't want either of us to live in poverty. I think she rather accepted that a wife's lot in life is a husband who engages in various affairs."

"Do you have any idea who the mother of this child could be?" Evelyn ran a finger down Perdita's cheek.

"I'm afraid not." Elise gestured towards her slim form. "I hope you can tell that it most certainly is not me."

"I do see that." Evelyn got up and walked over to the door. After a quick conversation with Malton, she returned to the room carrying the shawl baby Perdita was wrapped in when she was found. "Do you know who this belongs to?"

Elise looked at the garment, and a flush stained her pale cheeks. "It is mine. Where did you find it?"

"Perhaps the question should be where you lost it?"

"You can certainly ask me." Elise jumped to her feet. "But I will not answer you."

CHAPTER 6

*T*ommy didn't have far to look to find Fred. As he reached the end of the corridor where the ballroom was located, he heard the door close. He spun around just in time to catch sight of Elise going into the library.

Fred was sitting in the same chair he had used the previous evening. To his disgust, Tommy saw that the elderly man had continued to use the plant pot as his own personal ashtray.

"Northmoor!" Fred welcomed him jovially. "You join me again. Are you certain I cannot tempt you to join me in a cigar?"

It had been a long time since Tommy last smoked. The habit reminded him of his days in the Army. It wasn't something he had indulged in often since he returned home. Suddenly he craved a cigar. He walked over to the door, then asked over his shoulder. "Would you like a drink, Chesden?"

"Champion idea!" He replied with his usual enthusiasm. "Make mine a small brandy. Wouldn't do to get squiffy before dinner. Wife wouldn't like it."

Tommy couldn't imagine that Fred took much notice of what his wife liked. He opened the door and asked Malton to bring through two glasses of brandy and an ashtray. Sitting opposite Fred, Tommy decided that the best way to find out what he wanted to know was simply to ask.

"After dinner last night, did you remain in the drawing room until the police arrived?"

Fred laughed his usual boisterous bark of amusement. "Why don't you simply ask me if I killed the fellow?"

Tommy inclined his head. "Did you?"

"What possible reason would I have for doing that?"

It was an excellent question, and one that he and Evelyn had discussed earlier that morning. They had reached the conclusion that, so far as they were aware, there was no reason Fred, or his wife would kill Georges.

"I think I will take up your offer of a cigar, if I may?"

"I rather got the impression your wife does not approve of smoking."

"She does not have an opinion either way." Tommy reached out and took the cigar Fred offered. "I simply prefer the old way, where men smoke cigars after dinner in a room away from the women."

Fred passed matches to Tommy. "She's a fine-looking woman."

"I'm a very lucky man," Tommy replied, trying to keep the edge from his voice. "Evelyn is not only incredibly beautiful, but very intelligent. She does, however, have a terrible habit of singing around the house."

"Singing?" Fred frowned. "Whatever do you mean?"

The door opened and Malton brought in the requested drinks and an ashtray. He moved a side table over to sit between the two men.

"Malton, would you be so kind as to answer a question for me?"

"Of course, My Lord. How can I help?"

"How is my wife's singing?"

Malton's face was impassive, but Tommy knew him well

enough to notice a slight tightening of the butler's jaw "Singing, My Lord?"

"I was just telling Lord Chesden here about Evelyn's love of singing throughout the house."

"Her Ladyship seems to like a tune these days," Malton replied carefully.

"You have my permission to speak freely." Tommy grinned at the butler. "Singing is not one of Lady Northmoor's greatest talents, is it?"

Malton's expression did not change in the slightest. "I'm afraid not, My Lord."

"Thank you."

"Will that be all, My Lord?"

Tommy lit the cigar and inhaled. "Yes, I will call if we need anything further."

"How are you finding it?" Fred indicated the cigar.

Tommy laughed self-deprecatingly. "I must admit, I have gone quite lightheaded."

"Not used to it anymore, eh?"

"I have rarely indulged since the war," Tommy admitted, glad they were now talking about something aside from Evelyn. He was never comfortable when other men spoke about how attractive they found his wife.

"Terrible business." Fred shook his head. "Of course, my boys were both busy helping me run the estate. Neither of them saw any action. I suppose things were very different for you?"

It was another subject that Tommy did not like to talk about. He occasionally spoke to the local vicar, John Capes, who had helped him deal with some of his anger and distress following the things he had witnessed. However, no one could help him come to terms with what some of the things he'd had to do when serving King and country.

"I'm afraid so." Tommy took another pull on his cigar, then changed the subject again. "I asked earlier if you had stayed in the drawing room after dinner. Would you mind awfully answering that question?"

"Not at all," Fred replied. "As I intimated last night, my age means I visit the lavatory much more frequently than I did when I was younger."

Tommy wished he'd never asked. The last thing he wanted was to get stuck in a conversation about Lord Chesden's waterworks. "So other than to visit the necessary, you did not leave the room for any length of time?"

"That is correct."

"And your family?"

"I don't remember anyone leaving. You will have to ask them to be sure."

He had answered quite cleverly. He hadn't said that his family had remained in the drawing room, but neither had he ruled out the possibility that one of them may have left.

❧

*E*velyn knocked on the door to Victoria's room. "Aunt Victoria?"

Victoria came to the door. Evelyn hadn't seen her since the previous evening. She did not look at all well.

"You brought the baby again." She looked at Perdita with a curious mix of longing and dismay. "You had better come in. I am sure there must be lots of things you would like to ask me."

They settled in chairs next to the tall windows overlooking the street. In the private park opposite the house, Evelyn could see Doris walking Nancy and an excited Mary. All the houses around the square had access to the park via a locked gate.

"I'm not sure where to start," Evelyn said. "There are so many things that I would like you to tell me. After our last conversation, I have lots of questions. I don't know if you

71

will answer them all, but I would like to ask them all the same."

"Start at the beginning," Victoria said in a dull voice. "That is usually the best place."

Where, exactly, was the beginning? Was it something that happened in France? Did it occur when they first arrived in London? Or had whatever event set in motion the chain of events that led to Georges's death happened more recently?

"When did you and Lord Chesden decide to arrange a marriage between his son and your daughter?"

"He sent a note after Louis died. We have been corresponding for some months. The suggestion of a marriage between our children happened the first night we stayed at this house."

"Lord Chesden was aware of your address in France?"

Victoria lifted her chin haughtily. "You're not quite the little sweetie you appear to be, are you?"

"If you mean I am not taken in by fluff and nonsense, I shall take that as a compliment."

"I certainly meant it as one." Victoria held out her arms. "May I hold her?"

Evelyn stood up and passed the baby to Victoria. "Aunt Victoria, who is Gabrielle?"

Victoria closed her eyes. She pressed her lips tightly together as one did when trying to hold back the tide of overwhelming emotion. "I knew you would ask me that."

"And will you answer me?"

"Gabrielle was my daughter."

The swift maths that Evelyn had done in her head the previous evening came to the forefront of her mind. Victoria and Louis had been married forty years and yet had been childless for the first twenty of those. "Elise and Madeleine are your granddaughters aren't they?"

"I'm rather glad I didn't kill that boy." Victoria considered

Evelyn admiringly. "For if I did, I am sure that you would sniff out the clues immediately."

"If it is not too painful, will you tell me what happened to Gabrielle?"

"The agony never goes away." Victoria blinked away a sheen of tears. "Why do you think I drink? Do not be polite and deny that you either have not noticed or have not been told that in times of extreme stress, I drink to excess. I know I do it, but I cannot stop."

"I cannot imagine what you have been through." Evelyn looked at Perdita. "I have three nieces and two nephews. They are the closest I have to children of my own."

"Respectfully, Evelyn," Victoria said. "May I call you Evelyn?"

"Of course you may."

"Then you must call me Victoria and drop the aunt. It makes me feel positively ancient, and I'm not nearly as old as Aunt Em."

"I don't think anyone would dare refer to Em as old, especially not to her face. "

"She's exactly the same now as she was when I left England for France all those years ago. She is a very dear lady."

"Aunt Em did not tell me about Gabrielle."

Victoria raised an eyebrow. "Did you ask her?"

"I did not." Evelyn was not interested in having her deductions admired. Rather, she did not want Victoria thinking Aunt Em had been indiscreet.

"Evelyn, my dear. Having relatives that you love is a very wonderful thing, but it cannot possibly compare to having children of one's own." Victoria smiled. "I do not say that to be cruel, but simply to make you understand that a mother will protect her children above anything else in the world."

"Lady Chesden said something very similar to me yesterday evening. I do not take offence. It is no one's fault that I have yet to have children of my own. I cannot possibly allow myself to be upset that other women have experienced something that I haven't."

"I expect that rather puts Lady Chesden and me in the frame for this murder?" Victoria stared out of the window. "If we will both safeguard our children above anything else, then we would certainly murder to keep them happy or out of trouble."

Evelyn did not comment on the accuracy of that statement, even as she accepted its veracity. "I'm afraid I have something to tell you that may cause you some distress."

"There is very little that you could say that would shock me. Neither could you tell me anything that would hurt worse than losing a child. Gabrielle fell in love with a local boy. Before Louis and I knew what was happening, they had eloped and married. Two children later and, at the age of nineteen, my beautiful girl was dead."

Evelyn held a hand up to her mouth in horror. "Victoria, I am desperately sorry for your loss."

"So, you see, whatever it is you wish to tell me now could not be as bad as that."

"It's a very delicate situation," Evelyn said. "I am afraid that it has come to our attention that a clandestine relationship has developed between Hugh Norton-Cavendish and Elise."

Victoria shook her head. "In an attempt to prevent the girls from following in their mother's footsteps, I think I have been too strict with Elise and Madeleine. It has led both of them to be rather freer with their affections than is proper."

"You do not seem as surprised as I thought."

"My life has been very difficult. As a result, I am sad to say, very few things shock me these days."

"And Perdita?" Evelyn asked, nodding her head toward the child in Victoria's arms. "Who do you think she belongs to?"

"I believe she must be Madeleine's child."

~

ommy met with David Ryder after lunch. The young man looked keen to escape upstairs and avoid speaking to Tommy. With the key to the communal garden opposite the front of the house in his pocket, Tommy asked David if he would take a walk with him.

Reluctance radiated from David as he followed Tommy across the street. "I don't know what you think I can tell you."

"I have often found in cases like these people do not know how valuable information they may have can be." Tommy inserted the key into the padlock and pushed open the gate. Closing it behind them and re-securing the lock, Tommy pointed at a bench. "Shall we sit there?"

David shrugged. "I suppose."

"The police are convinced that the murderer is someone currently staying in the house. As you can imagine, that makes me incredibly uncomfortable because members of my family could be at risk."

David gazed at him levelly. "It is also quite possible one of those relations could be the murderer."

"You're right," Tommy said. "Obviously, it would be easier for me if it were someone else."

"I'm sure it would. Equally, I would prefer the villain to be someone in *your* family."

"I believe most of my family have very good alibis."

David gazed at Tommy with disbelief. "You cannot believe that. The only person I accept that you can vouch for is your wife."

"And I would hope we can both agree that it was not Aunt Em who killed Georges." Tommy wished he did not have to pit his family against the Ryders, but he could not think of any other way to encourage David to speak honestly to him.

"Your Aunt Victoria went upstairs for an extended period. Ostensibly to check on Elise who, as you know, had gone to bed early with a headache."

That was exactly the type of information that Tommy was looking for. Once the suspects all started turning on each other rather than giving each other a solid alibi, the pieces of the puzzle would slowly start coming together. "I will speak to my aunt. Your father has already told me he must make regular visits to the lavatory so also cannot account for all of his time between dinner ending and Georges being found dead."

"Father actually told you that?"

Tommy pulled an apologetic face. "I'm afraid that he did."

"I suppose the logical conclusion one would jump to considering what my brother said about Father and Lady Victoria is that they had a secret assignation," David said with a glum expression.

"I assume nothing without proof." Tommy watched a blackbird fly onto the grass to the left of the bench on which they sat. The bird plucked a small twig from the ground and flew into a nearby tree. How simple that little animal's life seemed to Tommy. Gather the necessary materials, build a nest, have a family. He would have to satisfy himself with collecting clues and solving murders, given that was what life had sent his way.

"I do not imagine the police will be so conscientious," David said. "This Price fellow seems like the type of detective who decides who the perpetrator is, then fits the evidence around his supposition."

"Do you think that because you have professional experience of the way some police handle their enquiries?"

"No, it is simply my own observation. My proficiency is

not in criminal law, but in business. I also do a little tax and estate planning for my business clients."

"Do you have your own office or are you with a firm of solicitors?"

"I work for Gold & Hampson here in the city."

That was a shame. Tommy had not engaged a regular solicitor since Westley Harrison. If David lived nearer, and was not a suspect in a murder enquiry, he would like to get to know him better with the view of engaging his services. "Do you have a particular reason for suspecting Detective Inspector Price will decide who the murderer is and then arrange the proof accordingly?"

"It was something in his manner when he questioned me last night. He already knew that I was romantically interested in Madeleine. Presumably my wonderfully loyal brother imparted that piece of information. The detective was very brusque and went so far as to suggest that he believed it likely that I killed Georges to eliminate the competition for Madeleine's affections."

"And you did not?"

"I did not," David confirmed. "In fact, I did not even know Georges was here in the house until the police told me he was dead. Until last night, I was not aware Georges even existed. In our conversations, Madeleine had never mentioned him."

"Do you know who did murder him?"

"Are you asking me if I know who has a better motive than I? Or simply who my own suspicions fall upon?"

Tommy held out his hands, palms up. "Either would be jolly useful."

"I can't help you, I'm afraid. The detective is correct in that I have the most likely motive for killing Georges. I don't know anyone who has a better reason for wanting him dead. I don't mind admitting to you that I am very fond of Madeleine. If I thought there was a chance of Father listening to me, I would plead with him that I step into Alexander's place and be the one to propose marriage to your cousin before Christmas."

"Surely your father would rather see you in a contented marriage with Madeleine than moving forward with a potentially unhappy arrangement between your brother and my cousin?"

David barked out a mirthless laugh. "You have had several conversations with Father now. He has gone so far as to share details of his toileting habits with you. Do you really think he is the type of man who is interested whether his children have happy marriages? His only concern is how our spouses might impact our family."

There wasn't much Tommy could say in response. The question wasn't how good a father Fred Ryder was. It was more how far David would go to get what he himself wanted. Was Fred so attached to the idea of Madeleine marrying his eldest son that he really wouldn't consider her as a wife for his younger son?

Tommy strongly disliked this stage of an investigation. They had some of the information that they needed and were learning more about the suspects and the dead person's life. However, there was still so much to learn. Experience had shown that when a murderer feels cornered, they will often strike again. A shiver ran down Tommy's back, as though his subconscious could feel the felon staring at him at that very moment.

It was a race against time to unmask Georges's killer before someone else became a victim.

CHAPTER 7

*E*velyn could scarcely believe it was time for afternoon tea. Despite the nap she and Tommy had taken earlier, she still felt so tired. It didn't matter that she remembered always feeling confused and lost in a sea of clues, lies, and secrets at this stage of a murder investigation. This time she was so exhausted she wasn't sure she could pick out the murderer even if he jumped up and down in front of her screeching 'It was me! It was me!'

The nursemaid had taken Perdita upstairs to be fed, and that led Evelyn to feel lost. The baby had been in Evelyn's life for less than twenty-four hours, yet her arms still felt empty without the baby snuggled in close.

Aunt Em poured three cups of strong tea into the blue-flowered cups sitting on a silver tray. Mrs O'Connell had also provided a selection of sandwiches. Evelyn's stomach rumbled as she realised she had missed both breakfast and lunch. She was suddenly famished.

Sarah Ryder leaned forward and picked up a sandwich. "How are you enjoying London, Lady Emily?"

"I am looking forward to Queen Charlotte's Ball. However, the older I get, the less appeal London has for me."

The ball was the most important part of the London Season, for it was at that event when the young ladies were presented to the King.

"You are keen to go home?" Sarah frowned, clearly puzzled. "You have only just arrived."

"I should say so," Aunt Em said. "But I suppose London has one particular advantage over Hessleham Hall."

"Oh, what might that be?"

Em looked critically at the sofa on which she was sitting. "The furniture here is remarkably clear of dog hair."

Evelyn giggled. "Em, really! It isn't that bad at home."

"You would sleep with those animals in their beds if Tommy allowed it, so you simply do not notice it."

Sarah looked aghast. "Would you really, Lady Northmoor?"

"Lady Emily is trying to lighten the mood. She knows very well I would not get into a dog bed despite my high regard for them."

"No, you would probably allow them to get into yours!"

"Surely you do not allow dogs upstairs in the bedrooms?" Sarah wrinkled her nose in utter disgust.

"Dogs are very useful," Evelyn commented. "For instance, they know when someone is moving about at night and alert their owner. When you live in a house with a murderer roaming free, I find their presence very reassuring."

"I can see how that would be so." Sarah shook her head slowly, clearly not convinced. "Personally, I cannot think of anything less appealing."

Evelyn lifted one shoulder in a slight shrug. "If the murderer knows my dogs are vigilant, perhaps he or she will not strike again."

"What makes you think they will strike again?" Sarah asked with a note of concern in her voice.

"Each murderer generally makes at least one mistake. They

may have been seen by someone near the scene of the crime, and that person is then in danger. Maybe a piece of information the murderer thought would remain hidden is suddenly discovered. They will kill to keep that quiet, so they are not implicated."

"That is why my nephew and Lady Northmoor have conversations like this," Aunt Em explained helpfully. "A person who has nothing to do with the murder would be only too keen to help."

"Do I take it from your joint lectures you think I have been holding back valuable information?"

"The murderer is either someone in your family or someone in my own," Evelyn said sensibly. "I completely understand no one wants to get their own relative in trouble. However, a man is dead. Whoever brought that event about deserves the punishment meted out by the court."

Sarah sighed. "What is it you actually want to know?"

"On the evening of the murder, did your family and Lady Victoria stay in the drawing room until the police came to inform you a crime had been committed?"

Sarah considered the question. Evelyn suspected she was concocting an answer. Although it was usual for someone to think about who had been where when recalling an incident, Sarah had plenty of time to consider this before now. "Lady Victoria went to check on her daughter. I don't remember anyone else leaving the room."

"Your husband has already admitted leaving on several occasions."

"Has he really?" Sarah laughed nervously. "How very bizarre."

"Bizarre because he did not leave or because he has already admitted the fact to my husband?"

"Fred has a very high level of self-preservation. I am simply surprised he has implicated himself." What a very upper class, polite way to say your husband was selfish.

81

Evelyn took a sip of tea. "I can't think of a single reason Fred could have for killing Georges."

"He's very desperate for Alexander to marry Madeleine."

"I imagine there are parents up and down the country frantic for one of their daughters to marry the Prince of Wales," Aunt Em said. "But few would contemplate murder to achieve their desire."

"As a motive, I agree it is very weak." Evelyn took a sandwich. "So you say Victoria left the room and agree that Fred also did so with some frequency?"

"I agree to the former, I do not agree with your latter suggestion."

"Even though your husband has given us that information himself?"

Sarah looked at Evelyn but did not answer. The only plausible reason she could think of for Sarah to be silent on the issue of Fred leaving the drawing room was because of the conclusions they would draw, because Victoria was also absent.

Was it also possible Sarah had left the room? Did she suspect, as Alexander had suggested, that Fred was once again interested in a relationship with Victoria? If so, where did that leave Sarah?

Evelyn had more questions running through her mind than answers. The only obvious thing was that the person with an obvious motive for killing Georges was still Victoria.

∼

*T*ommy ran toward the ballroom, where the sound of ferocious arguing reverberated throughout the ground floor of the house.

Frederick Ryder was pinned to a wall, his feet inches from the floor. His eldest son, Alexander, held him in place with an arm across his throat. "Alex!" David yelled from behind Tommy. "What are you doing? Release Father immediately."

"If he was spouting filth about your beloved Madeleine, you would be as angry as I am right now." Alexander moved his arm up and the gap between his father's feet on the floor increased.

Fred squealed, his face bright red. His eyes flitted between the different people in the room as though begging one of them for help.

Tommy sprang forward and released Alex's arm from where it was pinioning Fred to the wall. The older man shot him a grateful look, rubbed his neck, then slumped into a chair.

"What were you thinking of?" Tommy demanded

"It is not my fault," Alex said sulkily. "He is suggesting that Elise has taken Hugh to her bed. I will not listen to him slandering her character in that way."

"It's hardly slander, my boy, if it is true."

With a howl of anguish, Alexander rushed to his father and pushed him so violently both he and the chair toppled backwards. The back of Fred's head hit the wooden floor with a resounding crack.

Tommy winced. Where were the uniformed police that Detective Inspector Price had supposedly left in the house to keep them safe?

Sarah appeared at the doorway of the room. She rushed to David's side. "Darling, whatever is going on?"

"How very typical of you, Mother!" Alexander said scathingly. "Your husband is on the floor, I am in the process of trying to kill him, and all you care about is your darling David."

"Why must you always be so beastly?" Sarah gave a sob.

David moved away from his mother's attempted embrace and assisted Tommy to lift the chair and Fred from the floor.

"Are you all right?" Tommy asked.

"I'm going to change my will. I will write you out of it!" Fred fumed. "Just you see if I don't. I won't have it, Alexander, I simply won't."

"Do as you wish," Alexander said laconically.

"Fred? How are you feeling? Should I call for the doctor?"

Fred's colour had returned to normal. "I'm quite all right, Northmoor, stop fussing. Though I will take a brandy for the shock. And get your man to make it a large one."

Tommy walked over to the door where Malton stood hovering. "My Lord?"

"I think four brandies would go a long way to calming everything down." Tommy looked at Sarah. "Lady Chesden, would you like a drink?"

She shook her head. "I do not want a drink. I shall just go to my room."

Sarah fled from the room, weeping loudly.

"Maybe I should go after her." David looked after his mother with worry.

"For God's sake, David. Don't be such a wet blanket."

Tommy looked down the corridor. Evelyn was looking out of the door to the drawing room. "Don't worry, darling, everything is under control now."

He closed the door behind him and took a seat opposite Fred. David hovered near his father's elbow. Alexander prowled up and down behind his chair.

Malton returned with their drinks and quietly left the room. "You told your son what you had seen between Elise and Hugh? "

"He deserved to know. So I told him about that supposed friend of his and the Jezebel."

While Tommy could understand Fred wanting his son to know the truth and not be made a fool out of, he doubted that the man had an ounce of sympathy in his body. Alexander's extreme reaction couldn't only be at the news, but was more likely to be because of the way his father had told him.

"It isn't true, is it?" Alexander stalked around and stood in front of his father. "You have made this up so that I will do what you want and marry Madeleine. That's it, isn't it?"

"I have told you." Fred pulled out a cigar and matches. "I saw him in the library with that harlot. I shall not repeat precisely what I saw, but I can assure you they were doing something that was very inappropriate for an unmarried couple."

"I don't believe you. I simply don't."

"Perhaps you should just go ask him." Fred gestured towards the door. "Ask your long-time friend, the man we have supported financially for years while his father has gambled away the family fortune. Hugh goes everywhere we go and never pays a penny. Then he steals the girl you are interested in from underneath your nose."

Tommy didn't understand Fred's fervour. Why was he getting so involved when he hadn't shown even a slight concern for what either of his sons might want before now?

"I shall!" Alexander marched to the door and threw it open. It flew back on his hinges, then closed again with a loud bang.

"You've really done it this time, Father," David said. "You know how Alexander gets when he's in a rage."

Tommy raised an eyebrow. "How does your brother get when he is annoyed?"

David looked at his father. Fred stared back. Receiving no help, David picked up one glass and drank the amber liquid. "You saw how he was."

"That's not really an answer, is it? Does your brother often lose his temper and physically assault people?" Tommy pressed. David, as a solicitor, surely understood the implications of his brother's behaviour. After all, wasn't he the one who feared the police would jump to erroneous conclusions?

"Alexander struggles whenever he doesn't get something that he wants. All his life he has had whatever he wants. He's so very good-looking that most people are instantly charmed by him. If they happen to see through him and deny him what he wants, he has a tantrum a toddler would be proud of."

"Shouting and throwing things are not good behaviour traits for a gentleman. However, Alexander has gone a step further than that today. When I entered this room, he had to your father in some sort of chokehold. Goodness only knows what would have happened if we hadn't got here when we did."

"It's a family matter," Fred said decisively. "I shall take this matter no further. So don't involve yourself in our business and go looking for the police officer to report this. If they had been doing their job, they would have been here to see what happened. I will not be helping them by making a statement, so do not waste your time speaking to them about what you have seen."

Tommy copied David's lead and downed his drink. He took great care in placing the glass carefully on the tray when his frustration urged him to throw it into the fireplace.

~

*E*velyn kissed the top of Perdita's head. The baby smelled sweetly of milk, warmth, and a scent peculiar only to newborn babies.

She carried the child along the corridor to Madeleine's room and tapped on the door.

Gladys, Lady Emily's maid, answered the door. "Ah, Lady Northmoor. Miss Bernard has agreed to see you, My Lady."

"Thank you, Ferriby."

Gladys bobbed a knee as she always did. It did not matter how many times Evelyn told her she didn't need such courtesy, she could not persuade Gladys to stop. Evelyn moved into the room and sat in a chair next to Madeleine's bed.

The girl looked a little pale, but other than that, not unwell. She had obviously, and understandably, been crying and held a ferociously crumpled handkerchief in one hand. Her eyes darted to the baby in Evelyn's arms. "I didn't think you would bring her. Mother says you have been caring for her. I thought…that is, I believed, you would think I was a terrible person for abandoning my baby and tell me I could not see her ever again."

"She is your child," Evelyn said gently. "It is not for me to say what happens to her and whom she can or cannot see."

Madeleine reached out and pulled the blanket back from the baby's body. She put her finger in the little girl's palm. Perdita wrapped her chubby fist around her mother's finger.

It was over.

Evelyn's time of being the baby's caretaker was ending. Evelyn didn't need to ask Madeleine whether she intended taking over responsibility for her daughter. The answer was obvious in her expression.

"I'd forgotten," Madeleine said. "How could I forget? But somehow, I did. She's so very beautiful."

Everyone said the same thing when they looked at Perdita, and it was true. Some people said babies were beautiful, whether or not they were. But with Perdita there was no other way to describe her.

"Would you like to talk to me? About why you left her outside?"

"That's just it." Tears flowed down the young girl's face. "I didn't leave her anywhere. I gave her to her father."

"Perhaps we should start this story at the beginning, if that is all right with you?"

Madeleine sat up straighter in bed, winced, then smiled to cover her discomfort. "Would you mind terribly if I held her? For just a short time."

"My dear girl," Evelyn said. "She is your daughter. You must hold her for as long and as often as you would like."

Madeleine's face shone as Evelyn passed Perdita over. As Madeleine's pain ended, Evelyn's began. Madeleine's tears subsided as Evelyn struggled to hold hers at bay.

"I cannot thank you enough, Lady Northmoor, for caring for my baby so well. I'm so very grateful that she did not end up in the workhouse. If that had happened, perhaps we would never have been reunited."

Evelyn smiled as brightly as she could manage and hoped that it looked genuine. She was thrilled for Madeleine, but desperately sad for herself. The short time that she had assumed responsibility for Perdita only further reinforced her desire to be a mother.

"Now, you said you gave the baby to her father. Would that be Georges?"

"Yes, of course." Madeleine's eyes filled with tears. "I still cannot believe that he's dead. And worse than that, because someone has killed him. I can't think what could have occurred to bring about that result."

"When Georges came to the house last night, had you arranged to meet him?"

"I had sent a message to him. He was staying nearby. I suggested we meet near the gates to the garden when everyone had gone to bed. I wasn't expecting him to come into the house as he did."

"And what happened when he did?" Evelyn relaxed as the logical side of her brain took over. Analysing people, what they said, and their actions were safe things for her to do. They did not require any emotional input on her part. That was rather fortunate, as she had no more to give. "Of course, I saw him in the drawing room. But what happened after then?"

"He stayed in the stairwell that leads down to the kitchen. I met him there after dinner. I was quite certain that the baby would be born that evening. For obvious reasons, I had not told my mother. I saw a doctor in France, and he gave me some idea of what to expect."

"I wish we'd had a chance to get to know each other better. Perhaps then you would have trusted me with your secret and would not have had to give birth alone in this house. I cannot imagine how terrible that must have been for you."

Madeleine gazed adoringly at the baby. "It was quite dreadful. Much worse than I had expected. But I was not alone."

"Who was with you? "

"After dinner, I sneaked Georges upstairs to my room. I then came back downstairs for as long as I could possibly bear it. Then I made my excuses and returned to my room. Georges was marvellous and stayed with me the entire time. I couldn't have done it without him."

"Your sister said the shawl you wrapped the baby in was hers. She refused to tell us where she had left it. I would presume if it was in her room, she would have just said."

A look of shame passed over Madeleine's face. "I'm afraid I told Georges to creep along the corridor into any room and grab whatever he could find. Our plan was for him to take the baby to his lodgings. As soon as I could, I was to join him there, and we were to elope to France."

"Do you know whose room Georges went into?"

"I do not. Of course, I recognised the garment and knew it belonged to Elise. I didn't know that Georges would be killed, and it would look as though the baby was abandoned. Otherwise, Elise would just have presumed she had misplaced the shawl."

"So, the baby was born, you and Georges wrapped her in the borrowed shawl, then what?"

"That was the last I saw of either of them. Georges took the baby, intending to sneak out of the house. We knew it was tremendously risky, if someone had come out of the rooms he would have been discovered."

It seemed to Evelyn that was exactly what had happened. Someone had caught Georges, lured him outside, and then killed him. A dart of fury passed through her body. If that was correct, Georges had been murdered and the baby deliberately left outside where she most certainly would have died had it not been for Doris taking the puppy out one last time before bed. What type of person could do that to a defenceless infant?

CHAPTER 8

"Oh Tommy," Evelyn cried. "I knew we would find the baby's mother, I didn't doubt it. But I just couldn't help hoping. Wishing. Dreaming."

Tommy held his wife in his arms, heart aching along with hers. "I know, my darling. I know."

"It has been so easy for me to imagine Perdita in every room of Hessleham Hall. I can even see her lying on a blanket on the lawn on a sunny day."

"You had started to see her as your own child?" He spoke carefully, with no censure in his voice. It would be unspeakably cruel to point out that allowing herself to imagine something she knew could not happen was foolish.

Evelyn buried her head further into his chest. Her voice was muffled, but it did not lessen the deep pain he could hear in her every word. "I just wanted it so very much, but Madeleine is the child's mother. That is best for her and it is certainly best for Perdita."

Tommy winced as Evelyn spoke the name she had chosen. "Has Madeleine spoken about what she will call the baby?"

"I expect you think it would be better if Madeleine called her anything but Perdita. At least then every time she refers to the child using her new name, it will further remind me she belongs to Madeleine and not to me."

"I would prefer whatever brings you least pain. Though, of course, I wish you had not been hurt at all."

Evelyn lifted her head, plucked the clean handkerchief from Tommy's pocket and blew her nose with gusto. Her lips trembled as she gave him a weak smile. "We can't change what has happened, but perhaps we can find out what happened to Georges. Let us go through what we have learnt and see if we can make any sense of it."

It was pointless suggesting to Evelyn that she allow herself some time to come to terms with what had happened. Carrying on with their investigation into the death of Georges would distract her. If that is what she needed to do, he would wholeheartedly support her. "We know a lot more than we did before we went to sleep this morning, but I can't think of a single thing that actually advances our enquiries, can you?"

"I agree. More knowledge has not brought us any nearer to uncovering Georges's killer. Your aunt Victoria is still the primary suspect in my view. I still do not see a motive strong enough to cause any of our other suspects to commit murder."

"Fred is certainly unpleasant enough. From what I witnessed this morning, Alexander has a propensity for the type of violence that could lead him to kill someone. I don't like either of them one bit, but that doesn't make them murderers."

Evelyn went through to the bathroom to put the handkerchief in the laundry. Her eyes were red, her face blotchy. Still, she focussed on the puzzle they were discussing. "I don't think Elise and Madeleine know they are not Victoria's daughters. It's not the kind of question I could ask Madeleine, especially when she had just been reunited with her baby. I think that is something I should explore with Victoria. Perhaps there is a reason she has not told them."

"I think it is of great interest that Victoria and Fred kept up a correspondence over the years. Why would they do that? From Fred's point of view, a marriage was arranged between their fathers. Victoria and Fred themselves didn't have any sort of personal relationship." Tommy shrugged. "Or so he says. Maybe Victoria has a different take on the relationship?"

Evelyn sat on the corner of their bed. "Do we have any reason to suspect that is not the truth?"

"What are you thinking?" Tommy walked over to the bureau and pulled open the top drawer. He extracted a clean handkerchief and placed it in his pocket. He never felt fully dressed without a clean, pressed white hankie. "That there is a reason we have yet to uncover for Victoria and Fred to have written to each other for forty years?"

"In the mysteries we have solved in the past, there was always something that we did not know. People keep secrets from us. Otherwise, of course, they wouldn't be secrets, would they? Suspects especially have an excellent reason to keep confidences to themselves."

"Shall you speak to Victoria next?"

"Yes, I think there is more chance of her telling me about her history with Fred than Fred telling you." Evelyn sat in front of the mirror at the dressing table to repair her makeup. "I shall ask Aunt Em and Victoria to go to a tearoom with me. I would rather like to get out of the house. Hopefully Victoria feels the same way."

"What a wonderful idea, darling." Tommy walked over and stood behind his wife. He wrapped his arms around her and kissed her cheek before walking over to the door. "I will speak to Hugh and find out more about his alibi. He was sticking to the story that he was tired and alone in his room. I hope Alexander has not yet caught up with him. Though, I would hope the police have been rather more vigilant. I had a rather strong word with them after the incident in the library between Alexander and his father."

"You do that," Evelyn said. "And don't worry about me. I know you shall, but you really don't need to. I will be fine."

"Have a lovely time with my two aunts." Tommy wanted to say more, but now wasn't the time. If she wished to talk more about how she felt, she would let him know when she was ready.

Tommy left the room and wished an afternoon out would be enough to brighten Evelyn's spirits. They had come down from Yorkshire to get away from the things that were making her sad. He had believed a change of scene with different adults for company would be very good for her. Unfortunately, for lots of different reasons, that had not been the case.

What was the best thing for him to do?

He had thought previously that perhaps it would be a good idea for them to adopt a child. However, he hadn't wanted to suggest that to Evelyn in case she thought he said that only because he thought she could not give him a child. Now, seeing how she had immediately taken to caring for Perdita, he thought that might be the best way forward.

Something had to be done before Evelyn lost the spark in her eyes permanently.

❧

*O*ne of the uniformed police officers stopped Evelyn at the front door of the townhouse. He held up a hand. "I apologise, madam, but I have orders that no one is to leave this house."

Aunt Em stared at him so ferociously that he rubbed his hands together and shuffled his feet nervously. He looked over their shoulders as though hoping someone would come along and take over the responsibility of keeping the three ladies inside the house. "Do you have any idea whatsoever, young man, of whom you are addressing?"

The young officer flushed. "I do not. Neither do I know anything about you titled folk and how I should talk to you."

"Then let me assist you." Aunt Em stepped forward and drew Evelyn alongside her. "This is Lady Northmoor, her husband owns this house. I am Lady Emily Christie. With us is Lady Victoria Christie. We intend to walk along Belgrave Square to Wilton Row, where I understand there is a very satisfactory teashop near to the Grenadier public house."

"As I said, ladies, that is… Your Ladyships…" He frowned, clearly not sure he had used the correct form of address. "You cannot leave the house at this time."

"I have a solution for your dilemma," Aunt Em said. "We will allow you to accompany us. Of course, you will need to walk at least five paces behind us. It wouldn't be acceptable for you to walk alongside us. You may then stand outside the teashop and wait for us. From your vantage point you can ensure that we do not murder anyone, and that we ourselves are not murdered."

"I don't think…"

"Then don't think, young man." Aunt Em moved forward, and Malton opened the door for them, his face remarkably expressionless given the circumstances. She walked down the stairs and onto the pavement. "Come along. I clearly said five paces, not ten. Do keep up."

To Evelyn's surprise, the police officer did exactly as Aunt Em had told him to do. In less than two minutes, they arrived at the teashop. Em turned and fixed the police officer with a glare. "You are to remain where you are. You can see in through the window. I do not expect you to come inside unless it looks likely someone is about to attack us. If you can fulfil this very important task, you can be certain I shall contact your superior officer and let him know what a jolly good fellow you are."

When they were seated and had given their order, Evelyn turned to Aunt Em. "You were quite marvellous."

"Of course I was," Em answered without a trace of modesty. "I have had many years of practice causing ordinary people to turn into bumbling idiots by using my title and a particularly entitled tone of voice. Rarely do people challenge me."

A waitress hurried towards their table in a black uniform with a startlingly white apron over the top. The cap secured to the crown of her head was similarly bright. She placed a tray in front of them. "Would you like me to pour?"

"We shall manage quite well by ourselves, thank you," Evelyn said.

"I expect you are going to interrogate me again." Victoria waited until the waitress had moved away before speaking.

"I am sorry," Evelyn said. "There are some things that Tommy and I would like to clear up."

Victoria picked up a scone and bit into it. Cream oozed out onto the plate. When she had finished eating, she looked at Aunt Em. "I presume you are here to make sure that anything I say is historically accurate."

"You always did have rather a tendency to be dramatic, especially as a young girl." Em looked at her niece. "You were a very sweet child, but I remember exactly how things were in our family forty years ago, and I'm sure that you do too."

"You can't think that something that happened so very long ago has any influence on what is happening now."

Evelyn leaned forward in her chair and lowered her voice. "That is exactly what I think. Either you killed Georges to prevent him from eloping with Madeleine or there is some sort of secret or incident from your past that led to the murder."

"I can assure you, neither of your assumptions is correct." Victoria stared out the window at the police officer as though wishing he would come bursting in and rescue her.

"You said Lord Chesden wrote to you after the death of your husband. After that, you continued to correspond with each other until you met again at our home in Belgrave Square. Is that correct?"

"Goodness, Evelyn," Victoria said. "You sound incredibly official. Perhaps you could remember that we are family?"

"Perhaps you should remember that a young man has lost his life." Evelyn pushed the sugar bowl across the table toward Aunt Em. "You are the only person who has an actual reason to want Georges dead. If you would rather, we can go back to the house now and you can explain the nature of your correspondence with Lord Chesden directly to the police?"

Victoria fiddled with the bracelet on her wrist. "Are you certain the police suspect me?"

Evelyn sighed in frustration. "Who else has an obvious reason to kill Georges? I'm not saying that there are no other people in the house who could have a reason for wishing Georges dead. However, if that is so, their motive is currently unclear."

"Yes, we wrote to each other for some time," Victoria said at last. "As you pointed out earlier, for Fred to have written to me in France, he was aware of my address."

"I didn't ask you at the time, but I presumed that meant you had been corresponding for some time?"

"If you mean had we been in contact throughout my marriage to Louis, the answer is no." Victoria looked away. "In a moment of incredible weakness, I wrote to Fred and confessed how awful my marriage was. Fred wrote back a particularly well-worded letter full of compliments and claimed that he had never forgotten me, nor had he ever met anyone he admired as much as me. Apparently neither of his wives could hold a candle to me."

"You allowed yourself to fall for such nonsense?" Aunt Em asked.

"I'm afraid I did." Victoria blinked away tears. "As you know, I would have married Fred if I hadn't met Louis. When I wrote that first letter to Fred, Louis was in the middle of one of his affairs. I allowed myself to believe that if I'd married Fred, I would have had a happy marriage and Gabrielle would not have died."

"Forgive me, dear," Em said. "But you only had one child with Louis. Is there any chance that Gabrielle was Fred's child and that's why you contacted him when you were lonely?"

"Do you really think I would agree to a marriage between Madeleine and Alexander, knowing they were closely related?" Victoria shook her head. "I may have been very silly to have written to Fred and thought for even one single moment that he would have made me happy, but I would never allow that to happen."

"Yet there is something." There was no hiding the guilt on Victoria's face. "Something between you and Fred."

Victoria looked around the tearoom. "I wish we were somewhere more private. I feel rather exposed telling you my deepest secrets in public."

"I did not want us to be overheard in the house," Evelyn said. "However, I accept I didn't properly think through how very difficult this might be for you."

"Let us just get it over and done with," Victoria snapped. "I was stupid enough to meet with Fred on several occasions twenty years ago, both in France and in England. I am ashamed to admit that Fred and I indulged in an affair. I will never forgive myself. Not for being disloyal to my husband, though goodness knows he had affairs so many times in the past, but because if I had not been so busy with Fred, I may have noticed what was happening with Gabrielle right underneath my nose."

"Is there a chance Fred believes Elise may be his daughter?" Evelyn wondered, picking up on Aunt Em's earlier suggestion that Fred had some sort of hold over Victoria. "Is that why he was so keen to arrange a marriage between Alexander and Madeleine?"

Victoria sipped her tea. "He is blackmailing me."

"In what way?"

"He has kept much of our intimate correspondence. When Louis died, it is right that he wrote a letter of condolence. He also made it clear that if we were to return to England, he would expect me to become his mistress once more. When I refused, he said he would ruin me by *accidentally* allowing some of the more passionate letters I wrote to him to become public."

"So you agreed to a marriage between your granddaughter and his son to save your reputation?"

"Evelyn, respectfully, I have already said that you cannot possibly understand what a mother would do for her children. Since Gabrielle's death, Elise and Madeleine have been my children. If I were ruined in London society, they would be too." Victoria lifted a napkin to her face and dabbed at her eyes. "What was I to do? Have us all ruined or save the reputations of Elise and Madeleine?"

"You didn't answer the original question," Aunt Em said, concern and sadness in her voice. "Does Fred believe Elise is his daughter?"

"I don't know if that has even crossed his mind or whether he would care either way." Victoria shook her head. "But she certainly is not."

What a truly despicable man Frederick Ryder was. Evelyn wished there had been something in what Victoria had admitted that would implicate him in Georges's death, but there was not. If anything, Victoria's confession only solidified the case against her. She said herself there was nothing she would not do to maintain the reputation of both girls. Did that include murder?

"Sarah Ryder claims you left the drawing room the night of Georges's murder?" Evelyn asked reluctantly. "To check on Elise, who was feeling ill?"

Victoria looked thoroughly defeated. "Everything I say makes it look worse for me, doesn't it? I didn't check on Elise.

Of course, we now know she was with Hugh, don't we? I was looking for Fred to beg him not to release the letters. I was afraid that if he found out who Georges was, he would do it out of spite."

Victoria was right—there was nothing she could say that made her look less guilty.

~

*T*ommy eventually found Hugh. The police had listened to Tommy's admonishments that they needed to keep a close eye on Hugh as Alexander Ryder was looking for his friend and could not be trusted to have a civil conversation. They advised Hugh to lock himself into his room. One of the police officers stood guard outside. It wasn't the option Tommy would have chosen, but better Hugh be behind lock and key than be throttled by Alexander.

He knocked loudly on the door and called for Hugh to let him in. With great reluctance, Hugh opened the door wide enough for Tommy to enter.

"Lord Northmoor," he said. "How can I help you this time?"

"There are a couple of things that need clarification after our last conversation."

Hugh sat in one chair in front of the window. "I am locked in my room and I have just seen Lady Emily, Lady Victoria, and your wife walking down the street. It seems jolly unfair."

"I'm sure the police made it very clear to you that your life has been threatened." Tommy indicated the spare chair opposite Hugh. "May I sit down?"

Hugh lifted one shoulder in resignation. "It is your house, Northmoor. You must do as you wish."

"I apologise if you feel that the police have been rather heavy-handed, insisting you stay in your room for your own safety. However, I witnessed how furious Alexander was and was anxious about what he might do."

"I have known Alex for years." Hugh smiled. "He blows hot and cold all the time. One moment he is positively murderous, then the next as meek as a tabby cat."

"When we last spoke, you suggested Madeleine was involved with Georges. I didn't realise until later that you could not have known such a thing unless you had been told."

Hugh stared at Tommy, his jaw tightened, but he did not answer.

"I was then told that you were seen with my cousin, Elise, in a most compromising position. I therefore deduce that it was she who told you about her sister and Georges. Is that correct?"

"You are not the police. This may be your house, but I do not have to answer any of your questions. I refuse to say anything that may compromise that dear girl."

"Your denial rather answers my question." Tommy crossed one ankle over the other. "Though I admire your conduct in staying silent on the matter."

"Is that all?"

"Furthermore," Tommy continued. "During our previous conversation you suggested you were fond of a particular young lady. Would I be correct in thinking that is my cousin Elise?"

"I have not known your cousin for long, but she is particularly charming," Hugh said carefully.

"You were also honest enough to tell me that pursuing a relationship with a girl who has no family money would not be best for your family." Tommy folded his arms and looked directly at Hugh. "As Elise's nearest male relative, this leaves me in somewhat of a difficult situation. I have been told that there is a relationship of an intimate nature between you and Elise. You have very candidly told me that your family would require you to find a wealthy bride. Are you toying with my cousin until you meet someone rich enough to restore your family's finances?"

Hugh flushed and his plain face turned a mottled red. "Have I not just said how very much I admire Elise?"

"And yet you will cast her aside the moment a more suitable, *wealthy* young lady comes along?"

Hugh lowered his head and lifted a hand to cover his face. "You know how things are with my father. I have no choice."

"We always have a choice."

"You didn't want to be Lord Northmoor." Hugh's gaze fixed angrily on Tommy. "Did you ever contemplate turning down that position?"

"That isn't how it works," Tommy said, but he knew what Hugh would say next.

Hugh shook his head in disgust. "You inherited land, as I understand it, a beautiful old house that has been well preserved, and wealth. You might not have chosen your title and everything that goes with it, but you accepted it as your duty. If I do not marry for money, I cannot keep my family estate running. I do not wish to be the one who loses everything."

"Is that not your father's responsibility?"

"Of course it is." Hugh's voice was full of frustration. "Everyone knows how it is his gambling that has cost our family its fortune. But will anyone remember that when it is me who will be left after he's gone, having to sell everything including our family home? Once he's dead, I will still be here dealing with the shame."

"And Elise?" Tommy asked quietly. "Does she know this?"

"We have spoken about my family situation." Hugh gazed out of the window. "Elise understands my position."

"Is there no one in the wider family who can assist?

Have you asked a solicitor to go through your grandfather's will? Perhaps there's…"

"David has checked," Hugh responded in a defeated voice. "There's nothing except the trust. It provides an income for my father's lifetime. I'm not sure how much will be left for mine. His inheritance is gone. Generations of our family have lived at Rochester Park."

It wasn't Tommy's business, and he shouldn't interfere, but he felt desperately sorry for the young man. "Has David given you any advice?"

"He suggests selling parcels of land to raise money but, of course, Father would never agree to that. I don't have the heart to tell him it's much too late to keep up appearances. Everyone knows how his gambling has crippled us financially."

"Your mother?"

"Sadly, she is no longer with us. My sister, Emma, hardly dares to leave the house because of the embarrassment. There's no money for her to have a Season. It's a desperate state of affairs."

Tommy hated pressing Hugh when things were so difficult for him, but he still needed answers. "Were you and Elise together all night after leaving the drawing room?"

"You would like me to alibi myself, and your cousin, by admitting she was in my room?"

"Not that it matters," Tommy said. "But it is my understanding that you were in her room."

Hugh shook his head in astonishment. "How could you possibly know that?"

"Elise's shawl was used to wrap the baby. She admitted she had misplaced it. Therefore, it was not in her room. It must have been taken from your room, so it follows that you cannot have been in there with Elise."

"I had no reason to kill that French fellow."

Tommy admired the other man's steadfast refusal to admit

Elise had been with him, despite the evidence of the contrary. "I shall have to take your word for that given you have no one to vouch for your whereabouts around the time he was killed."

He got to his feet and walked toward the door. "Northmoor?"

"I care for Elise very much."

"Thank you for your time, and your honesty."

Tommy wished there was something he could do, but he knew from experience how much money it took to run a large estate.

CHAPTER 9

"*I* rather think you could have asked me if I wanted to join you." Elise pouted. "I would like to have got out of the house."

"We had some things to discuss," Victoria said to her daughter. "Very private and personal things."

Elise shook her head in disgust. "So you chose two people, one whom you have not seen for years and one whom you have never met before yesterday, to speak to rather than your own daughter."

"Evelyn has some more questions for you." Victoria moved over to sit next to Elise on the sofa. "After she has finished, I will tell you everything we have spoken about. You are quite right, darling, I should talk to you more often."

"If you are going to ask me about my shawl again, I will still refuse to answer you." Elise addressed Evelyn. "It is none of your business."

Victoria patted Elise's hand. "I know I cannot understand because of the secrets I have been keeping. But you really should tell the truth. If you were not involved in Georges's death, please just answer Cousin Evelyn's questions."

"What secrets?" Elise asked.

"There are many things that I have hidden from you and your sister. Today, I will change that. Please talk to Evelyn first."

"I left my shawl in Hugh's room." Elise stared defiantly at Evelyn.

"Goodness," Aunt Em said. "I think I will require a large gin if we are to speak of such matters."

Victoria got to her feet and went over to the drawing-room door. Malton followed her back in and asked each of the four ladies present if they would like a drink. No one declined.

"Malton," Evelyn said.

"Yes, My Lady?"

"It is one of those days when I believe we all require a long pour of gin."

"Of course, My Lady," he replied. "Short on the tonic?"

"Very short." Aunt Em winked at Evelyn.

"I don't believe we had such excitement over drinks when I lived at Hessleham Hall." Victoria smiled at Em and Evelyn. "Is this a recent change?"

"There are days," Aunt Em said. "When Evelyn and I scandalise Malton with the size of our afternoon tipple."

Malton moved around the room serving drinks and moving side tables so they all had easy access to their glass. As soon as he had left the room, Evelyn looked at Elise. "Please forgive me for asking such an impertinent question, but it is very important. Were you with Hugh the night Georges was killed?"

"Yes, I was. He met me in the library. We kissed quite passionately in that room, as I recall."

"Are we to have a blow-by-blow account of every little thing you and Mr Norton-Cavendish did that evening?" Em asked.

"I wasn't planning on it," Elise responded. "Unless you would like every single detail?"

"If you are trying to shock me, my dear," Aunt Em said. "You will find that quite impossible."

"I believe it was during that encounter when you were seen by Lord Chesden." Evelyn raised an eyebrow at Elise.

The girl looked away and finally looked embarrassed. "He told you that?"

"Lord Chesden told Tommy, who then tried to clarify this with Hugh. He was the perfect gentleman and would reveal nothing other than to state that he was very fond of you."

"Doesn't matter how much he likes me. In bed or out of it. I'm poor and he needs a rich wife."

"My dear girl, I do hope you only speak like this because you feel comfortable in front of us because we're your family. Away from us, you must learn some discretion," Aunt Em admonished.

Elise took a sip of her drink, coughed, then stared at the clear liquid. Finally, she seemed to relax. "This is very strong."

"And after you were in the library?" Evelyn prompted.

"We went upstairs. To my room."

"You were together all night?"

"Yes, we were." Elise lifted her chin defiantly, as though she expected someone to challenge her outrageous behaviour. She took another mouthful of her drink and blinked rapidly, as though trying to prevent her eyes from watering.

"Thank you," Evelyn said. "It is so very important that we know exactly where everyone was. We can then narrow down our suspects."

Elise looked at her mother. "Don't you have anything to say?"

"None of us are perfect." Victoria leaned forward and kissed Elise's cheek. "I haven't been to church in years, but I vaguely remember there being something about a sinless person casting the first stone upon a sinner. I am not without immorality and therefore cannot, and will not, judge you."

"What about you?" Elise asked, looking at Aunt Em.

She no longer looked sulky but like a child who was desperate for the adults in her life not to castigate her because of her quite outrageous actions. Aunt Em was successfully downplaying her reaction to Elise's attitude, but there could be no denying spending all night in a man's room was shameful.

"Your mother is correct. We are all sinners, dear." Aunt Em looked at the glass in her hand and chuckled. "I'm certain the Lord would disapprove of Evelyn and I taking our strength from a large gin rather than meaningful prayers."

Evelyn knew Aunt Em's words were correct. When was the last time she had prayed for strength in dealing with adversity? Perhaps she had been praying for the wrong thing. Instead of asking for the Lord to send her a baby, she should ask for peace and acceptance with her life just how it was.

∾

*A*lexander Ryder stalked around the library like a caged animal. "Did you know the police have locked Hugh in his room?"

"I did," Tommy said calmly. "In fact, I told them to keep a close eye on him for his own safety."

"Hugh and I have been friends for years. I would never do anything to hurt him. He certainly knows that."

Tommy smiled. "Hugh actually referred to you as a tabby cat."

Alexander pulled a hand through his already unkempt hair. "You see? I'm jolly angry he made a play for Elise. He knew I liked her."

"Did you?" Tommy raised an eyebrow. "Did you really like Elise or was your interest in her because your father was pushing you at Madeleine?"

Alexander grimaced. "I suppose it was a little of both. I

was angry that my father did not give me a choice. He is a very controlling man. If there is something he wants, he always gets it. For once, I wanted to choose for myself."

"Is that why you calmed down quickly?"

"Yes, it wasn't that my feelings for Elise were strong. I suppose, if I'm being honest, I also felt rather embarrassed that she would choose a chap as plain as Hugh over me. He is a splendid fellow, we are close chums, but even he admits himself that he was towards the back of the queue when good looks were being handed out."

Tommy still did not trust Alexander. The fury on his face as he was attacking his father was still too fresh in his mind. However, he had a measure of sympathy for the man. His cousin, Eddie, had grown up to be a bully and believed he could do whatever he wanted to whomever he wanted and get away with it because he was the son of an earl. He didn't doubt that Eddie was a product of the way he had been raised by his father. The similarities between Eddie and Alexander were clear for Tommy to see.

"On the night Georges was killed, did you stay in the drawing room with your parents and Lady Victoria all evening until the police arrived?"

Alexander assessed Tommy coolly. "None of us were there the entire time."

"Is that so?"

"I don't see the point in lying any longer. Why should I protect anyone but myself? Nobody else has concern about anything but their own interests. I intend to do the same."

"Where did you go?" Tommy moved over to the brandy decanter. "Can I pour you a drink?"

"I rather think I've had enough already." Alexander indicated the empty tumbler on the table. "I went to look for Elise. I knocked on her bedroom door, but there was no answer. It seems quite obvious now that she must have been with Hugh."

"And Victoria?" Tommy pulled out the stopper from the neck of the decanter and poured a small brandy. Instinct told him it was important at this stage of the investigation to keep his wits about him.

"She said she went to check on Elise. It is only right that I tell you she was gone a long time. My father was not in the room at the time. When Lady Victoria had been absent for around ten minutes and neither she nor my father had returned, my mother went to look for them."

"What about your brother?"

"Saint David?" Alexander scoffed. "My perfect brother alleges his shoes were pinching his feet, so he went to his room to change them. However, I am not as stupid as he believes me to be. When he came back downstairs, he was wearing the same pair."

Tommy contemplated his next question. He thought Alexander had been honest so far. The information that he was sharing was very useful, and he wanted that to continue. "Do you think it is at all possible that David killed Georges?"

"Of course it is possible," Alexander replied. "I think, in certain circumstances, we all have the propensity to commit great violence. However, do I believe my brother killed Georges? No, I do not."

"On what do you base that belief?"

"I suppose on years of knowing my brother. I am the eldest son, I received most of my father's attention. David never once showed any jealousy or signs that he resented my position in the family."

"Could he have been so angry when Georges came to the house that he killed him?"

"Because of his affection for Madeleine?"

Tommy sipped his drink. "Yes."

"He has known her a very short amount of time." Alexander flopped into the chair opposite Tommy. He no longer looked frustrated, but rather sad. "I do not believe that brief acquaintance would elicit the sort of fervent emotion one would need to kill a love rival."

Tommy agreed. Alexander himself had shown that he was prone to flashes of temper, David had not. Was it possible that the younger brother had hidden depths? Of course it was. He thought back to the case they had solved earlier that year. The murderer on that occasion had been a rather insignificant person, not at all the type of character one would imagine capable of intense passion.

It was important that he did not remove anyone from the list of suspects simply because they appeared to be an agreeable person.

~

Evelyn asked to speak to Sarah before she went up to get changed for dinner. The other woman was extremely reluctant. "Oh, Lady Northmoor, really? How tiresome."

"Tommy and I have found out some additional information since we last spoke. It is only fair that I ask you what you think."

"That really is not your responsibility."

"Lord Northmoor and I see it as our concern. Not only did the murder happen in our home, the perpetrator must be one of our friends or family. That knowledge affects us both deeply."

Sarah Ryder twirled a closed fan around in her hands. "I don't see that I can help you. And before you send Lady Emily to speak to me about how I should answer your questions if I am innocent, do not bother. This whole incident is clearly to do with Lady Victoria and her family."

"That may be so," Evelyn said. "However, as well as Lady Victoria, your husband also left the drawing room. I know also that both of your sons did too. Alexander claims to have been looking for Elise and told us that David had left to look for Madeleine."

"Whoever told you that must have been mistaken." Sarah patted her brown curls. She was an attractive older woman, but not nearly as striking as Victoria. "That is not how I remember events at all."

"How do you remember them, Lady Chesden?"

Sarah looked up as if she was concentrating deeply to remember what had happened less than twenty-four hours ago. "After dinner, we all came through to the drawing room. I recall a lot of wine was served with dinner. Several people had imbibed before they ate and then had copious amounts during the meal. It is my opinion that quite a lot of your guests, Lady Northmoor, were drunk."

"That does not differ from any ordinary evening," Evelyn said. "It is very possible everyone had too much to drink. But what do you remember happening that was out of the ordinary?"

"Absolutely nothing." Sarah tapped the fan on her knees.

This was incredibly hard going. Evelyn wanted to shake the answers out of the other woman. "In the drawing room, it is my recollection that Malton served many more drinks. Tommy and I were very tired following our journey down from Yorkshire, and we went to bed early. Aunt Em retired at the same time as us. My question is: What happened after we went to bed but before the police arrived?"

Sarah looked bored. "The same as always. Fred talked too loudly, Lady Victoria flirted shamelessly with him. My sons were terribly embarrassed, and I just sat there and put up with the unacceptable behaviour as I have for years."

"Did you yourself leave the drawing room?"

Sarah's eyebrows rose in surprise, but Evelyn could not tell whether it was genuine or an act. "What reason would I have to do that?"

"Is it perhaps because your husband and Lady Victoria

had been absent for some length of time?" Evelyn looked carefully at Sarah, but she could not detect any emotion on the other woman's face. "Is it possible you were afraid they were sharing a tender moment?"

Sarah barked out a laugh. "I'm supposed to care if Fred and Lady Victoria are involved again?"

"Again?"

"Oh yes, again." Sarah tapped the fan against one leg, the only sign of her agitation. "Of course again! If Fred does not wish me to find out about his peccadilloes, he should make a more concerted effort to hide his personal correspondence."

"Goodness," Evelyn said. "I am most terribly sorry."

"Why are you sorry? It has absolutely nothing to do with you. I have always been aware that I was not the great love of Fred's life. He was married before me. That poor girl probably died of a broken heart. She was very young. No doubt she believed all of Fred's declarations of love, but that man loves nobody but himself."

"Don't you believe he loved Lady Victoria?"

"Absolutely not," Sarah sniggered. "I'm sure she believes Fred's dalliance with her is the only one he has ever had during our marriage. I mentioned his first wife. It is my belief that his behaviour appalled her so much she simply could not cope with the shame of it."

"What happened to her?"

"I never asked what exactly happened to her. She died. That's all I know." Sarah blinked and her face, which had been unusually animated during her speech about her husband, now returned to its usual blank expression. "So, you see, I didn't need to leave the drawing room because I have always known what Fred is."

Evelyn wanted nothing more than to go upstairs and lay her head on a pillow and sleep until she was fully rested. Why was Sarah so adamant she hadn't left the drawing room when Alexander had been very clear that she had? Was she hinting that something untoward had happened to Fred's first wife?

"Thank you for talking to me."

"May I go now?" Sarah got to her feet. She did not wait for a response but walked swiftly out of the room without a backward glance.

Evelyn was more confused than ever. Sarah was an incredibly odd woman. There could be no doubt she'd led a difficult life, but her abrasive tone made it difficult to feel any sympathy for her.

CHAPTER 10

*T*ommy found Fred in the ballroom before dinner.

"Ah, Northmoor." Fred inhaled deeply on his cigar. "This visit has been an absolute disaster. We will leave first thing tomorrow."

"Do you have clearance from Detective Inspector Price for that?"

Fred waved a dismissive hand. "I shall worry about that. Don't you interfere."

"As you wish." Tommy sat in the chair opposite. "It has been a rather eventful twenty-four hours."

"Eventful?" Fred spat. "It has been an unmitigated debacle. A murder, an illegitimate birth, copulating youngsters all over the house. Frankly, I am disgusted."

"Is it your opinion that it is more acceptable for the older generation to fornicate than it is for the younger?"

Fred coughed loudly, cleared his throat, then slowly and deliberately tapped cigar ash onto the floor. "What do you mean by that?"

Now was not the time to prevaricate, plain speaking was required. "Both your wife and my aunt Victoria have intimated that there was a secret relationship between you and

115

Victoria approximately twenty years ago that you were hoping to rekindle."

"Not that secret if they have both told you."

"I will assume the information I have received is correct."

"Assume what you like." Fred leaned back in his chair and stared at Tommy with open hostility. "What I did, or did not do, twenty years ago has no bearing on the events in this house."

Tommy had to concede that Fred rather had a point there. If Fred had been the victim, there would have been many viable suspects, but what possible connection could there be between Fred's past and Georges's death? "What happened to your first wife?"

Fred's face turned red, and he blew out a stream of smoke. "What has that got to do with anything?"

"I'm really not sure," Tommy said. "Maybe nothing, but perhaps everything."

"I will answer, but only because I have absolutely nothing to hide. My first wife died after falling from her horse. If someone has insinuated that there was something sinister in her death, then they are obviously trying to cause trouble for me."

"So it had absolutely nothing to do with your promiscuity?"

Fred barked out a sarcastic laugh. "I'm not sure where your moral compass is, Northmoor after what has gone on in this house. Who are you to be judging me?"

"It is necessary to ask troublesome questions when you are trying to unmask a killer."

"Perhaps you should leave that to the professionals." Fred tilted his head. "What promiscuity are you referring to, as a matter of interest?"

"I have been told, and apologies if this is incorrect, that over the years of both of your marriages you have habitually kept a mistress. You even admitted to me last night that you enjoyed your time between your first wife and Sarah."

"There is nothing wrong with a chap enjoying the company of a woman when he is single," Fred said pompously.

"So you did not have a relationship with Victoria at the turn of the century?"

Fred considered his answer and eventually sighed deeply. "Victoria is different. She has always been special to me. For years, I expected to marry her. As a result, I have remained fond of her over the years."

"So fond you were amenable to a marriage between your son and Victoria's daughter?"

"I thought they might succeed where we had failed." For the first time, Tommy could see genuine emotion on Fred's face. It vanished almost as soon as it appeared. "Of course, Alexander will not be marrying that strumpet of Victoria's now."

"I'm sorry to hear that." Tommy was nothing of the sort, but he had run out of things to say to Fred.

"What are you talking about, man?" Fred wagged a finger at Tommy. "Not only has that girl been sinful, she has done so with some foreigner who ended up getting himself killed. It is an absolute disgrace that my son has been under the same roof as her."

Tommy breathed deeply through his nose before answering. "I hardly think it was poor Georges's fault that he was killed."

"Perhaps if he hadn't been indulging in an illicit relationship with that girl, he would not be dead," Fred said emphatically.

"Do you think that's why he was murdered?"

"It seems rather obvious to me," Fred mumbled. "He turns up, his harlot has his child, then someone kills him."

"How do you know it is his child?"

Fred shook his head. "I suppose it could be someone else's. If she is easy with her favours with a French man, I suppose she could have been just as easy with someone else."

Tommy got to his feet. He wasn't learning anything new from Fred and being in the same room with such a horrid man was trying what was left of his patience. He hurried from the room before he said something that he would later regret.

～

"David, might I have a word?" Evelyn stopped him as he was about to go upstairs to change for dinner.

A distinct lack of enthusiasm radiated from David but did not stop him answering politely. "Of course, Lady Northmoor."

"I'm sure you've heard the news about Madeleine?" she said as she closed the library door behind them.

David looked down at the brightly patterned carpet. "Father told me that the abandoned baby is hers. I cannot deny that I am feeling very despondent."

"I'm afraid that is correct," Evelyn said. "Were you very fond of her?"

"I think I was falling in love with her," David admitted. "I'm certain that with a little more time, I would have fallen completely head over heels for her."

"What will you do now?"

David didn't pretend to misunderstand. "Father has insisted we all leave tomorrow. We will go to our London house and Alex and I will continue the Season there. I expect Hugh will come with us. Of course, he and Alex have made up. They have been chums for such a long time, it would take much more than a girl to come between them."

"I believe Hugh is very fond of Elise."

"He most definitely is." David nodded. "I think that made it much easier for Alex to forgive him. Hugh has genuine feelings for Elise, Alex did not."

"What a terrible shame that Hugh's family finances will come between their romance."

"I fear it will. I'm afraid Hugh's father has depleted their bank balance so catastrophically there can be no way out for the family and no happy ending for Hugh and Elise."

Evelyn walked over to a chair and sat down. It was barely evening, and she was already wishing she could retire to bed. "How very sad. Is there nothing they can do?"

"They have an awful lot of land on their estate in Derbyshire. Perhaps if Lord Clifford, Hugh's father, were to sell some of the land, that would go some way to funding the estate for a few years. I understand from Hugh that he is not willing to do that."

Evelyn considered him. "Are you very knowledgeable about the running of large country estates?"

"I spent a lot of years learning how our own estate was run. I don't know if you know, but I studied law at University and I practice in business and estate planning. Obviously, estate planning is about organising one's financial affairs, particularly for the next generation, but I think my background is particularly useful in advising clients who have large country estates. I understand it because I have lived it my entire life."

"How fascinating." Evelyn agreed with Tommy. It would be very useful to have someone of David's calibre to advise them on the running of Hessleham Hall. How she wished she didn't have to ask him where he had gone the previous evening at around the time Georges was killed.

"I always think explaining what I do sounds incredibly boring." David looked away self-consciously. "But I find it incredibly interesting."

"I can certainly see why Tommy admires you so much. He

also finds such talk fascinating." Evelyn leaned forward in her chair. "May ask you something personal?"

"Is it something about the investigation?"

"It is," Evelyn confirmed. "Does that change whether or not you will answer me?"

"I am an honest man." David walked over to stand near Evelyn's chair. "I have nothing to hide."

"I understand you left the drawing room last night to change your shoes?"

David lifted his chin slightly. "That is correct."

"And did you change them?"

He frowned. "What do you mean?"

"You left the drawing room, you went upstairs to change your shoes, did you actually change them? That is what I'm asking you. You went to do a particular task, but it seems that you did not complete it."

"Someone in the drawing room was particularly obser-vant last night." David spoke without a hint of frustration. "I said that was what I was going to do. I actually wanted to speak to Madeleine."

"And did you?"

David looked away. "The truth is, Lady Northmoor...I did not."

Evelyn stared at him for a long moment. It seemed to her that he was going to say something else and changed his mind at the last second. She understood why Tommy found David such a likeable fellow, but that didn't change her strong suspicion that the thing he was going to say was that he had seen something the previous evening he wasn't expecting. And that was a man leaving Madeleine's room.

❧

*A*s Lord Chesden left the ballroom, Tommy saw Doris coming down the stairs with Nancy and Mary. "I don't suppose you could find someone to tidy up in there, could you?"

"Of course, Lord Northmoor. What is it that needs doing?"

"I'm afraid Lord Chesden is not as careful with his cigar ash as we might expect."

"I will see to it at once." Doris walked along the corridor, then turned back, a frown on her face.

Tommy held out his hands. "Pass the dog leads to me. I will watch them while you find a maid to clean the mess. "

"Yes, My Lord."

As Doris walked past the library, Evelyn came out with David. He looked at the dogs. "What beautiful animals."

"They are rather, aren't they?" Tommy agreed.

As Evelyn walked towards them, both dogs pulled on their leads. "Hello girls, have you missed me?"

Two tails thumped on the floor in unison. David laughed. "I think that means yes."

"Shall we wait in here for Doris to come back?" Tommy suggested pointing towards the ballroom. "See you at dinner, David."

David gave a wave as he walked towards the stairs.

As soon as they entered the ballroom, Nancy threw back her head and howled. Tommy looked at Evelyn as Nancy shivered whilst keeping up the mournful sound.

"I remember the last time she made that sound."

Tommy grimaced and looked around the room. "So do I."

The previous autumn, the local member of Parliament had been found dead in the stream at the edge of the lawn at Hessleham Hall. Nancy had reacted to either the dead man or the scent of his blood. Evelyn bent next to her dog. She stroked Nancy's head. "What is it?"

"I don't think she's going to tell us."

Evelyn threw Tommy a stern look. "Now is not the time for jokes, Thomas Christie!"

"The police have been in here. They searched the entire downstairs of the house when I realised my letter opener was missing. I'm pretty certain they searched upstairs whilst we were sleeping."

"Well, either they have missed something, or something has been placed in here after their search."

Doris returned and looked at them both quizzically from the door. "What is wrong?"

"We are not sure," Evelyn said. "Would you see if you can find one of the police officers? Could you close the door on the way out, please?"

Doris nodded and hurried out of the room.

"Shall I take off the lead?" Tommy looked at Evelyn.

"Yes, I think you should."

Nancy trotted over to a plant pot near some chairs. She sat in front of the aspidistra and continued to howl.

Tommy hurried over. "Do you think there is something in there? Other than Fred's cigar butts, of course."

"How absolutely vile," Evelyn commented. "Couldn't he find an ashtray?"

"I don't think he's particularly bothered that someone has to clean up after him." Tommy peered into the soil at the base of the plant. "I can't see anything."

"Don't touch!" Evelyn admonished.

The door opened and one of the police officers followed Doris into the room. "What is all that din?"

"My dog is extremely sensitive," Evelyn said. "I have reason to believe there is something in this plant pot upsetting her."

The policeman surveyed the aspidistra and then pointed at it. "Might it be this plant?"

"Where is the Detective Inspector?" Tommy demanded. "It is extremely important you get him here immediately."

"For a plant?" The policeman asked with a frown.

"For a murder weapon," Tommy said urgently. "Now, where is he?"

A loud scream sounded from the corridor, followed by a series of sickening thumps as someone tumbled down the stairs.

CHAPTER 11

*E*velyn rushed from the ballroom to the foot of the stairs with Tommy close behind her. Hugh lay on the stone tiles with an alarming puddle of blood pooling around his head. She looked up the stairs. Had he tripped and fallen? She dismissed that idea almost as soon as it had formed. The scream had sounded before Hugh tumbled down the stairs. It was a cry of pure terror.

"Everyone move back!" the policeman from the ballroom shouted dramatically.

"I shall call for Detective Inspector Price and an ambulance." Tommy hurried off to the telephone.

"Doris, take the dogs and find Mrs Chapman. Ask her to give you some towels and a warm blanket. As quick as you can."

The policeman took out his whistle and blew into it. At once another policeman appeared at the top of the stairs. The front door opened, and another officer stepped into the entranceway.

"What happened?" shouted the constable as he hurried down the stairs.

"Fell, pushed, or jumped. I just don't know."

Doris hurried back with an armful of towels. Evelyn took one and felt around Hugh's skull until she found where he was bleeding from. She pressed the towel firmly against the wound.

"Here!" The officer stepped forward and put his hands on Evelyn's shoulders. "What are you doing? You can't touch him. He's evidence."

"This man is a victim. If I can stem the blood, perhaps I can keep him alive until help arrives. Surely you would prefer a live casualty to another dead body?"

His hands slid down Evelyn's arms, and he pulled her away from Hugh. Nancy lunged forward and sunk her teeth into the bottom of his trousers. The policeman yelped in surprise. "Get that animal off me!"

Evelyn moved back into position and recommenced pressure on Hugh's injury. "Nancy, drop."

Nancy immediately let go of the constable's trousers. "That dog is vicious!"

"Don't be so ridiculous," Evelyn said. "She was clearly protecting me as you were manhandling me across the floor. Keep your hands to yourself or next time I shall let her bite you properly."

"Goodness, what have I missed?" Tommy asked as he returned.

Evelyn glared at the policeman in question. "This fool tried to stop me from helping Hugh. As you were not here, Nancy stepped in to protect me."

"Hugh!" Elise hurried down the stairs, stopping on the last one. "Is he dead?"

"No," Evelyn said. "I can see his chest moving. He is definitely breathing."

"What happened?"

"I don't know." Evelyn shook her head. "Tommy and I

were in the ballroom. We heard a shriek and then a series of thuds as Hugh fell down the stairs. Goodness only knows what has happened."

"Obviously somebody has tried to kill him!" Elise screeched. "Why would somebody want to kill Hugh? I just don't understand."

"Try to stay calm," Tommy said soothingly. "Nobody knows what has happened yet. It's possible it's just a terrible accident."

"I don't believe that for a moment," Elise cried.

Evelyn didn't either. She thought somebody had given Hugh an enormous push from the top of the stairs. Like Elise, she couldn't imagine why anyone would do such a thing.

The front door opened again, and Dr Michaels came in carrying his medical bag and quickly assessed the situation. "Did he fall the whole way down?"

"There were no witnesses to the event," Tommy said. "We heard the commotion and came running, but nobody knows exactly what happened."

"Have you sent for an ambulance?"

"Yes," Tommy replied. "I have also informed the detective in charge of the murder enquiry that there has been an incident. He is on his way."

"I will examine him as best I can." The doctor shook his head. "It's a very serious injury. It may be best that we do not move him from the house, the journey to the hospital could well be too much for him."

"Oh, please don't let him die," Elise said. "I will do whatever I can to help him. Please let me help him, doctor."

"If you are going to stay calm and not faint, I shall let you stay." Dr Michaels said to Elise. "Everyone else should leave this area immediately."

Evelyn got to her feet and followed Tommy back to the ballroom. Doris took the dogs toward the servant's stairs. She couldn't begin to make sense of what had happened. Was it possible Victoria had gone mad and was attacking any men who showed an interest in her granddaughters? Had Alexander pretended to forgive Hugh? David had only just left to go upstairs. Was there some reason he had attacked Hugh? Elise was the only person to come out of her room. Could she have been so upset after talking to Victoria that she had struck Hugh in frustration, knowing he would not marry her because she was poor?

There were many more questions than answers, and another of their guests lay gravely injured. Why couldn't they make sense of the clues they had?

~

Tommy got to his feet as Detective Inspector Price came into the ballroom.

"I thought I told you two to stay out of my investigation!" he raged. "Now what is this nonsense the constable is saying about something in a plant pot?"

"My dog reacted very badly when she came in here," Evelyn explained. "There must be something in with the plant."

"Your dog?" he asked sceptically.

"She howled and sat next to the aspidistra over near those chairs." Evelyn pointed. "She has only behaved like that on one other occasion, and that was when there was a dead body on our estate in Yorkshire."

His eyebrows rose. "There was a dead body on your country estate?"

"Yes, he'd been murdered."

"Then you come to London and somebody is killed. Don't have much luck, do you?"

That was putting it mildly, Tommy thought. They had

absolutely rotten luck. "Are you going to check the plant pot?"

Price shook his head as though unable to believe he was trusting a dog's natural instinct as he walked over to the aspidistra. "Maybe she doesn't like cigar butts?"

Tommy raised an eyebrow. "Please check properly."

The detective poked around with his fingers for a few moments. He turned, looked at Tommy in surprise, then returned to his task. Seconds later, he drew out the letter opener missing from Tommy's desk.

"Does this belong to you, Lord Northmoor?"

"Yes, it is the letter opener I previously informed you was missing."

Price walked to the open door, holding the item away from his body. Even though the blade had soil adhering to it, dried blood was still visible. "Watkins, get in here right now!"

One of the uniformed officers hurried in. The detective pointed at Tommy. "Arrest him!"

"Lord Northmoor?" the officer replied in surprise.

"Yes, him. Immediately."

Tommy shook his head and held out his wrists. "I suppose you will want to put me in handcuffs?"

"You are being arrested for murder, Lord Northmoor. Of course you need to be cuffed."

"Is this really necessary?" Evelyn asked. "We *found* the murder weapon. Why would we lead you to it if Tommy had killed Georges? Not to mention he has no motive."

"Lady Northmoor, please do not tell me how to do my job."

Tommy watched as his wife stepped toward the detective and jabbed a finger into his chest. "I shall if you are doing it badly."

"Do you want to be arrested for assault?" he snapped. "If so, carry on."

"You're making a terrible mistake," Tommy said quietly as he worked hard at keeping a hold on his temper.

"Why? Because you have fancy titles?" Price sneered. "I would happily arrest the King if I believed him to be guilty of a crime."

"No," Tommy said. "Because I have done nothing wrong. Maybe it would be worth your while telephoning Detective Inspector Andrews of the North Yorkshire constabulary? He will confirm to you we have assisted on investigations in the past."

"Harrington." Price pointed at his colleague. "Go make that call. As for you, Watkins, get those handcuffs on him and sit him in one of those chairs while I decide what to do with him."

No sooner had Watkins read Tommy his rights and snapped the metal rings closed around his wrists than the infuriating tap of a cane in the corridor outside the ballroom announced the impending arrival of Fred Ryder. He was the last person Tommy wanted to see him in such an undignified state.

The tapping got louder, and Fred finally entered the room. "Oh dear. What *have* you done?"

"Found the murder weapon the police couldn't. So in a fit of spite, they arrested me."

"Really?" Fred raised a disbelieving eyebrow. "Seems rather implausible to me. This really has been a most remarkable stay. I think I will go to my club tomorrow. The chaps will think this is a quite hilarious lark."

"It is hardly a laughing matter," Tommy said through gritted teeth.

"I suppose that all depends on where you're standing."

Tommy wished, rather uncharitably, that Lord Chesden would suffer from a nasty case of gout. If Fred had his way, half of London would know Tommy had been arrested before lunch.

"Watkins, clear this room!" Detective Inspector Price barked.

"I've come in here to smoke," Fred said belligerently. "Where can I smoke if not in here?"

"Outside," Tommy hissed.

As Fred left, another uniformed officer came in. "The doctor doesn't think the gentleman who tumbled down the stairs has any broken bones. He's bandaged the fellow's head and says he wants to move him upstairs where he will stitch the wound. It's his belief it could be dangerous to move him to the hospital."

"Fine. You guard the door. At least until we find out whether he was pushed or simply had a little too much afternoon whiskey or whatever it is he drinks." Price waved an uninterested hand, then seemed to realise he was still holding the murder weapon in his other hand. "Watkins, send someone in here immediately to take care of this dagger or whatever it is. And find Harrington! How long does it take to make a telephone call?"

"Please try to calm down," Evelyn said. "You're looking quite red in the face."

The detective whirled around to face Evelyn. "Comments like that will not help to keep me calm, Lady Northmoor."

"I'm sure," she murmured. "I have a plan that I think might help with that."

"How many times do I have to say it? Do not seek to involve yourself in an official investigation!"

The door opened once more, and another uniformed officer and Harrington came in.

"I'll take that, sir." The officer held out his hand.

Tommy sighed. "There's a clean handkerchief in my pocket. Perhaps you could use that if you want to preserve any fingerprints there may still be?"

He stood up, and Evelyn extracted the white hankie and

passed it to the officer, who took the letter opener and hurried from the room.

"They have done this sort of thing before, and had a high degree of success," Harrington interjected.

"This sort of thing?" Price snapped.

"Investigating," Harrington replied. "Andrews said they are 'frustratingly diligent' but he couldn't deny their ability in uncovering several murderers."

"Provincial police don't know what they are talking about," Price muttered as he glared at Tommy. Harrington leaned forward and whispered something into Price's ear.

"Would you like to hear my plan now?"

The detective shook his head in bewilderment. "I don't suppose it would hurt. Can things possibly get any worse?"

"Why don't you *forget* to station someone outside Hugh's room after dinner?"

"What sort of proposal is that? Why would I do such an unprofessional thing? I don't know how your Andrews fellow does things in the country, but we carry out our investigations properly in London."

"The murderer won't know you've actually hidden police officers *inside* Hugh's room."

Price opened his mouth to say something, then closed it again. Eventually he gave a slight nod. "That could work."

"It's an excellent idea," Tommy said. "Why don't you spread the word at dinner that they have taken me to the station, Evelyn? It's possible that will cause our murderer to lower their guard because they will think they have escaped detection for the murder."

"What makes you think you're not going immediately to the nearest police station?"

"If you intended to do that, you would've had me transported by now," Tommy said calmly. "Now, why don't you stop blustering, come and sit down, and let's work on Evelyn's plan together."

~

*L*ater that evening, as the clock in the hallway chimed eleven, Tommy and Evelyn waited in their bedroom for news that their plan had been put into effect.

Over dinner, Evelyn had spoken loudly about how Hugh had recovered from his terrible accident. She had told everyone that although he was still very poorly, he was sitting up in bed and talking. While he couldn't remember exactly what had caused him to fall, the doctor was confident that he would remember in time.

"I wish Price had let me hide in Hugh's room. I'm furious to miss out on all the action."

"I think we're jolly lucky he allowed you to stay in the house. There was a point this evening when I was convinced he would have one of his officers take you away."

Tommy grimaced. "Me too. I so wanted to be there to apprehend the perpetrator personally."

"Sadly, you're stuck here with just me." Evelyn smiled at him.

"I can think of worse places to be," Tommy said in a low voice. "Why don't you come over here next to me?"

Evelyn got up from the bed and moved over to their bedroom door where Tommy was standing with one ear pressed against the door. "The wood is so thick, you'll hear nothing through it."

Tommy stood behind Evelyn and wrapped his arms around her. He nuzzled her neck. "I don't think I care about the murderer anymore."

"Well, I do. A person with such obvious mental imbalance must be locked away where they can do no further harm."

"Must you talk about such things when I am preparing to whisper sweet nothings into your ear?" he groaned.

She twisted in his arms and reached up to press her lips

against his. "Plenty of time for that later, Tommy. Let's concentrate on more important things."

Despite Evelyn's words, it wasn't long before they gave up their vigil at their bedroom door and crawled into bed. Their lack of sleep caught up with them and they fell into an exhausted sleep.

CHAPTER 12

"*You* slept through the entire thing?" Aunt Em asked incredulously.

Evelyn laughed, a little embarrassed. "I'm afraid we did. Though I'm not sure how hard Detective Inspector Price tried to wake us."

"I should expect he wanted to take the credit for solving the murder all to himself."

Malton brought through the tray of coffee and placed it on the sideboard. Breakfast had been a meal of absolute necessity. No one wished to spend any more time than was necessary in the dining room when Tommy and Evelyn had promised to reveal how they had uncovered the murderer as soon as everyone had finished eating.

"You know that doesn't bother either of us," Evelyn said. "All we care about is the police have taken the villain to prison where he belongs. Hugh has genuinely regained consciousness now, and the doctor is hopeful of a full recovery, though he will need to spend some time here with us before he is well enough to travel to his own home."

"Of course, we should remember that although the events

of the last two days have been tragic, we have a new family member that we wish to celebrate." Tommy walked over to where Madeleine sat on a sofa holding her baby and bent to kiss first his cousin and then her child. "Evelyn and I are proud that Madeleine has asked us to be baby Josephine Emily Gabrielle Bernard's godparents. We are currently working on persuading Madeleine to have the baby christened in our local church in Hessleham."

"Cook has been spoiling Madeleine these last couple of days. I rather think that the promise of a few months of Mrs O'Connell's fabulous meals will win her over. What do you say, Madeleine?"

"I say yes." The young girl smiled at Evelyn. "How could I say no? You and Cousin Tommy have ensured that Georges's killer will not escape justice. For that alone, Josephine and I will be forever in your debt."

"Why must you do all the sentimental things first?" Aunt Em demanded. "There's plenty of time for that at the end, when you've told us how you worked all this out. I must admit that even though I know who did it, I'm still completely flummoxed."

"Patience, Aunt Em."

"I'm an old lady," she said grandly. "I don't have time for patience."

Tommy poured coffee as Evelyn settled herself into an armchair. "Elise, shall we start with you?"

"I didn't have a motive, did I?"

"No, you did not. We knew that immediately but, of course, we cannot rule you out simply because we did not know what your motive could be. However, it was quickly apparent that you liked Georges very much and were saddened by his death. Even though you were not completely honest with us from the beginning, we understand why that was. We hope very much that you will come with your sister and Josephine to Hessleham, where you would be most welcome to stay with us for as long as you would like."

"That is very kind, but Hugh is going to need somebody to nurse him back to good health. We haven't actually spoken about this yet, but I do hope that he will let that person be me."

Tommy passed Elise her coffee. "Perhaps his family would agree to him convalescing with us? Just a thought. Why don't you speak to Hugh and then let Evelyn and I know what you both think to that idea?"

Elise jumped to her feet and remembered to place her cup on a nearby side table before throwing her arms around Tommy. "Oh, Cousin Tommy, you really are the best cousin I've ever had!"

"He's the only cousin you've ever had experience with," Madeleine said with a laugh. "It would be marvellous for Josephine and me to have you with us too."

Elise returned to her seat. "I rather think that Hugh would benefit from some time away from his responsibilities and family duty."

Evelyn turned to Alexander. "It was very difficult for us to think of a reason you could possibly have for killing Georges. Although your father was keen to arrange a marriage between yourself and Madeleine, both you and David told us plainly that was not what you wanted."

"I was very worried about the anger you showed towards your father," Tommy admitted. "You showed a flash of temper that encouraged me to believe that you could commit murder. You also accepted that, in certain circumstances, it is possible that anyone could be moved to murder."

"I was too busy looking for Elise to be in the kitchen killing that poor French boy," Alexander said, then shrugged. "Complete waste of time that was, of course."

"Moving on. Sarah, you were a tough person to interview.

You didn't want to tell us anything and refused to confirm things that others had told us. We thought it was very possible that you could have killed Georges because you made it clear on several occasions that there was nothing you wouldn't do to secure your children's happiness."

"David had become very fond of Madeleine. Until I was aware of her rather promiscuous ways, I had believed she would make an excellent solicitor's wife. I would not have murdered someone, simply so my son could marry the woman of his choice. There are limits to what a parent should do for their child."

Evelyn wished Sarah did not feel the need to be so downright rude to Madeleine, but she could understand the other woman's reasons.

"Aunt Victoria, you were our primary suspect from the very beginning. There was absolutely nobody with a better motive than you. Georges reminded you of your husband and you wanted better for your girls than a life of poverty." Tommy smiled at his aunt, who sat between Aunt Em and Madeleine.

"Let us call my girls what they are." Victoria smiled at Elise and Madeleine. "They are the children of my darling daughter, Gabrielle. I could not love them anymore if they were my own daughters. I'm very proud of them both and have high hopes for their future."

Evelyn thought Victoria had been very brave in sharing information with Elise and Madeleine. She had told the girls absolutely everything, the truth about their mother, that their father had left Gabrielle when Elise was very young, and finally about their mother's death.

She turned to the last remaining person in the room. "Finally, David, you also had an excellent reason to want Georges out of the way. In the short time that you have known Madeleine, you had become very close to her."

He shook his head sadly. "I know Alex said that anyone has the potential to become a murderer, in certain circumstances, but I disagree. There are some people that just do not have that in their personalities. I could never kill another man."

"I'm not sure if you would be interested in this, but I have a proposal for you." Tommy handed David an envelope. "You can read this later, but the gist of my letter is that I would very much like you to come and work in Hessleham. I have a need for a solicitor that I can trust to help me and my estate manager. I also have a business proposal that I hope you will be interested in. Brief details are at the end of my letter."

David looked at Madeleine, then back at Tommy. "That is a very kind offer. I will certainly give it a great deal of thought. Thank you."

"And so," Evelyn said. "The person who killed Georges was Frederick Ryder, the Earl of Chesden."

"We both realised this shortly after we found the murder weapon in the ballroom," Tommy added. "I presumed Fred had shoved the letter opener into the soil in the plant pot after killing Georges."

"Aunt Em actually helped in solving this murder. If she hadn't made a comment to Elise and me about how noisy Fred's cane was, I might not have suggested to the police that they look inside."

"Inside?" Aunt Em looked puzzled. "Whatever do you mean?"

"One of my father's friends had a similar cane," Evelyn explained. "It has a removable ornamental top and is hollow. He kept a supply of cigars inside, so wherever he went he always had a cigar on hand. We realised that whoever committed the murder could not have simply killed Georges and then walked back through the house. The letter opener would have been dripping with blood."

"It was actually rather ingenious," Tommy said. "After the

murder, Fred simply put the knife into his cane and then transferred it to the plant pot as soon as he was alone in the ballroom."

"He made one error," Evelyn went on. "When I spoke to David before dinner yesterday, he told me his father had informed him that the abandoned baby belonged to Madeleine. At that point, no one outside of our family knew that. The only way Fred could have known is if he had been the one to catch Georges trying to leave the house with the baby."

"But how did he know anything about Georges?" Aunt Em wondered.

"You're right. He wasn't in the drawing room before dinner on our first evening here when Georges came in. However, he arrived shortly after Madeleine took Georges down to the kitchen. If you remember, he made a comment about Madeleine and what a strange setup we have here."

Madeleine gasped and covered her mouth with a hand. "He must've seen us."

"Seen you, what do you mean?"

"When we came out of the drawing room, just before we got to the servants' stairs, Georges kissed me. Do you think it's possible Lord Chesden witnessed that?"

"I'm afraid so," Tommy said "He then left the drawing room several times after dinner on the pretext of needing the lavatory. Finally, on one of those occasions, he met Georges coming down the stairs carrying the baby."

Victoria looked at her youngest granddaughter. "Darling, do you really want to hear this?"

"I rather feel as though I should. I owe it to Georges, and one day I will have to share with Josephine how her father died. Although it will be very painful, I would rather hear it for myself now."

"We believe Georges headed towards the servants' stairs, either thinking Fred wouldn't follow him or, more probably, there would still be somebody awake downstairs." Tommy paused. "The only person who really knows what happens next is Fred. We know Georges was found with part of a fifty-pound note in his hand. We think Fred tried to pay Georges to leave with the child. Possibly Georges took the money before he realised Fred meant forever."

"You don't think Georges had accepted the bribe?" Madeleine wiped her eyes. "If he had the money, perhaps he just took it."

"If he accepted it," Tommy said. "There would be no need for Fred to have killed him. Almost certainly, Georges took the money, then refused to abandon you. Fred then killed him and snatched the money back from Georges's grasp."

"How positively dreadful," Em commented.

"It certainly will be for us left behind," Sarah lamented. "No one in London will receive our family after this."

"I hardly think that compares to this poor girl losing the man that she loves, and her child's father being murdered," Tommy said sharply.

"It's certainly true that it'll be jolly difficult for me to find a wife now," Alexander said morosely. "Mother is right. No respectable family is going to want to be anywhere near us. We will be social outcasts."

Neither Sarah nor Alexander appeared to realise that things were going to get much harder for their family in the coming months. There would be a trial and if a jury found Fred guilty, he would hang. The shame of that would be very much worse than how they were feeling at that moment.

"How did the police catch Fred?" Victoria asked.

"We almost forgot that!" Tommy exclaimed. "The police wanted to leave a guard outside Hugh's door in case the murderer tried to finish Hugh off after Evelyn told you all at dinner that he had regained consciousness and it was only a matter of time before he remembered what happened and could identify who pushed him."

"I persuaded them to hide police officers inside the room to see if Fred, because we knew that was who it was, would return," Evelyn explained. "He did and attempted to smother Hugh with a pillow."

"But why?" Elise cried. "What had Hugh done wrong?"

"Fred was desperate for Alexander to marry Madeleine. I think it reminded him of when he was to marry Anne, but she died and so he was then to marry Victoria. If Alexander couldn't have Madeleine, then Fred decided he would make sure Alexander could have Elise."

"Are you suggesting that Father went a little mad?" David asked.

Tommy lifted a shoulder. "We can't possibly know whether the balance of his mind was affected, or if he simply pushed Hugh out of spite."

"I believe Fred never stopped loving Victoria. Sarah, you tried very hard to persuade us that Fred had many affairs over the years, but you never could come up with a reasonable explanation why you left the drawing room when your husband and Victoria did. I think he simply tried to ensure his sons succeeded where he himself failed," Evelyn suggested.

"I suppose it is too early for us to have a celebratory drink?" Aunt Em asked hopefully. "I do think we should admire your marvellous sleuthing."

Evelyn shook her head and glanced at the clock in the corner of the room. "It is barely ten in the morning. It is most certainly too early."

"Perhaps this evening we could have a special dinner in remembrance of Georges and to rejoice in the safe arrival of our darling Josephine," Tommy suggested.

"That seems an adequate suggestion," Aunt Em said. "After all, it's not every day one has a great-great-niece named after them!"

"It's not every day a person lives long enough to meet a great-great-niece." Tommy laughed.

"Enough of that young man!" Em wagged a finger in his direction. "You might be a jolly good detective, but that is no excuse for being cheeky to your elders."

Tommy walked over and kissed his aunt on the cheek. "You love me just the way I am."

Not even Aunt Em had a suitable response.

❧

*A*fter they had finished talking through the resolution with their family and guests, Tommy and Evelyn went through to the library.

Tommy sat heavily in the chair behind the desk. He ran a hand over the space where he had kept his letter opener. "If Price tries to return the murder weapon, I shall not accept it. I don't want that thing in this house ever again."

"Of course not, darling. Are you really going to open those letters now?"

He looked up at her and raised a quizzical eyebrow. "Why? What do you have in mind?"

Evelyn pushed Tommy's hands off the desk and climbed onto his lap. "I thought we could just sit here and enjoy each other's company for a few minutes."

"I like that suggestion very much."

"Tommy, are you still looking at those letters?"

"There's one from my mother," he said in a distracted voice. "How strange she would write to me here in London."

"She knew we were coming down here. What's odd about it?"

"The letter must have been sent before we left Yorkshire." She could hear the frown in his voice.

"Alright," she said resignedly. "You may open *one* letter. Then I will not ask for your full attention, I will demand it."

Evelyn rested her head on Tommy's chest and closed her eyes. One of the principal reasons they had come to London was so she could escape the babies at home in Yorkshire. She soon realised that holding her new nieces or hearing about Isolde's pregnancy did not make her pain worse—being absent from those she loved did.

It had been her suggestion that they offer Victoria, Elise, Madeleine, and Josephine a home at Hessleham Hall. If being an aunt and a godmother was the closest she ever got to holding a child of her own, she would do her very best to be content with that.

"Mother is getting remarried."

Evelyn blinked then struggled to twist in Tommy's arms so she could face him. "Helen? Married?"

His lips twisted. "I see now why she mailed this letter to London. She expected us to be here for some months."

"I didn't even know she was ready for remarriage."

He shrugged. "It has been over three years since Father died. But, no, I didn't know. Neither my sisters nor brother have mentioned that anyone has been calling regularly."

"Do we know the man?"

"She doesn't say what he is called. Only that he is the Marquess of York."

"Goodness." Evelyn wished she could think of something more intelligent to say but for once in her life, she was speechless. Tommy would be crushed. He had adored his father.

He threw the letter onto his desk. "She has asked that we host the wedding."

"The wedding and the guests? I don't understand."

"At the chapel on the grounds of the manor," he replied in a flat voice. "And yes, the guests are all to stay with us."

"But…" Evelyn paused, trying to find the right words. "Isn't it a little unorthodox to marry one's second husband at the home of the first husband's family?"

"That's certainly one way to put it. The question is: Will we do it?"

THE END

MURDER IN THE WEDDING CHAPEL
COMING AUGUST 2021

CLICK HERE TO PRE ORDER

A NOTE FROM CATHERINE

Thank you very much for reading *Murder in Belgrave Square*! I had so much fun writing this story, and I very much hope you enjoyed reading it. If you did, please consider leaving a review. Not only do reviews help other readers decide if *Murder in Belgrave Square* is a book they might like to read, but they also help me know what readers did, and did not enjoy, about my book.

If you would like to be amongst the first to know about my new releases, please join my monthly newsletter via my website.

I have also formed a Facebook group for fans of cozy mysteries. It's a place where we can chat about the books we've read, what we like about cozies, TV programmes in the cozy genre, etc. It is also the place where I will share what I'm writing, price drops, but most of all letting readers know about FREE ARCs that are available. You can also find the link for that group on my website.

www.catherinecoles.com

Printed in Great Britain
by Amazon

78523247R00089